THE
CHICKEN
FARM
FIASCO

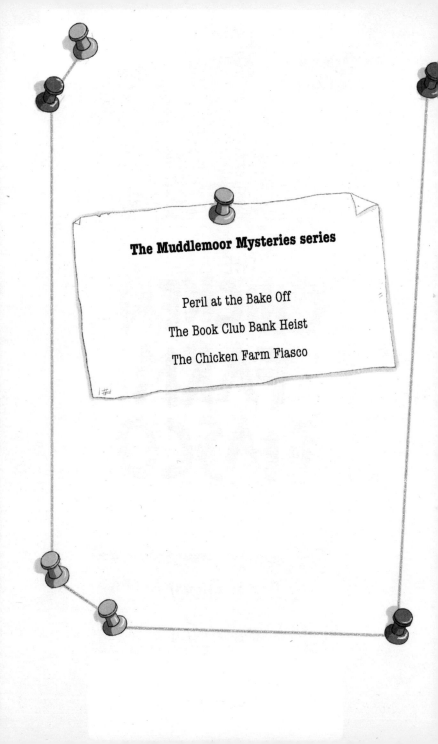

The Muddlemoor Mysteries series

Peril at the Bake Off

The Book Club Bank Heist

The Chicken Farm Fiasco

THE
MUDDLEMOOR
MYSTERIES

THE
CHICKEN
FARM
FIASCO

by Ruth Quayle

illustrated by
Marta Kissi

Andersen Press

First published in 2023 by
Andersen Press Limited
20 Vauxhall Bridge Road, London SW1V 2SA, UK
Vijverlaan 48, 3062 HL Rotterdam, Nederland
www.andersenpress.co.uk

2 4 6 8 10 9 7 5 3 1

British Library Cataloguing in Publication Data available.

ISBN 978 1 83913 255 1

Printed and bound in Great Britain by Clays Ltd, Elcograf S.p.A.

For Charlie,
number one plot-untangler.
– RQ x

For my husband James,
with all my love
– M.K.

MUDDLEMOOR VILLAGE

STONELY

ALLOTMENTS

THE GRAVELS...

VILLAGE HALL

PLAYGROUND

OLD TENNIS COURT

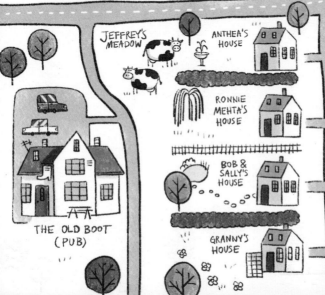

JEFFREY'S MEADOW

ANTHEA'S HOUSE

RONNIE MEHTA'S HOUSE

BOB & SALLY'S HOUSE

OLD OAK

STREAM FARM

THE OLD BOOT (PUB)

GRANNY'S HOUSE

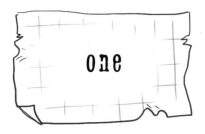

one

This is a story about the Easter holidays, except it has nothing to do with chocolate eggs or fluffy bunnies or roast lamb.

It has a teeny amount to do with chicks, but not in a good way.

I can't tell you the whole plot straight away because I don't want to ruin the story. Once, my mum's friend Suzy told me the whole plot of a book I was reading and after that I didn't fancy reading it any more. Mum's friend Suzy is always telling me about books that are 'wonderful' but 'wonderful' books are not my favourites. I prefer ones that are gripping and funny.

Hopefully this book will be gripping and funny but, right now, all I can tell you is that it is about the Easter holidays. Actually, that's not quite right either, because it's not ABOUT the Easter holidays, it's just about what happened during them. It is quite a dangerous story. It is a bit shocking.

Normally I love Easter. For one thing, I am mad about chocolate (even the dark sort that makes you thirsty) and for another thing, at Easter I always go to stay with my granny in Muddlemoor (Muddlemoor is the name of her village. It is in the countryside). This year I was even more excited than usual because my cousins, Tom and Pip Berryman, were staying with Granny too. Me and my cousins often stay with

GRANNY

Granny in the school holidays when our parents are working. Granny says we get on like a house on fire. She says this like it's a good thing but I don't know what is so good about a house burning down. Once, I tried explaining

JOE ROBINSON

this to Granny but she burst out laughing and said, 'You lot and house fires have plenty in common – you're both **EXTREMELY** destructive!' And then she said, 'Scallywag!' and gave me a hug.

This year's Easter was anything but normal. It was actually quite scary. Not just 'hands over your eyes' scary or 'can't go to the toilet on your own' scary (which is what happens when me and my cousins watch *Jaws* without a grown-up) but a bit scarier than being sent to the headteacher's office for a 'chat'. And **WAY** scarier than when our burglar alarm goes off in the middle of the night (lots of things make our

TOM AND PIP

3

burglar alarm go off in the night, including spiders, and I'm not *too* scared of spiders because they are living creatures and I love all living creatures, except maybe cows).

Luckily, me and my cousins are used to dangerous situations when we are staying with Granny in Muddlemoor. The first time we stayed with her on our own, we discovered that one of her neighbours was SPYING on her with a robot spy cat. Since then, things have got worse. Last time we went, we had to protect her from the police AND a gang of bank robbers. Nowadays, we are used to having to start our own investigations to stop Granny getting in trouble. Sometimes we get in trouble ourselves.

But if you haven't read about our previous investigations, don't worry. All you need to know is that Muddlemoor is a hotspot for crime. You should also probably know that Granny is lucky to have us around to keep an eye on things, even if she doesn't realise it.

I don't mind that Muddlemoor is a hotspot for crime because whenever I am there I have Tom and Pip to help me out. Tom and Pip are way cleverer than the children at my school and they are also good at using their initiative. Like for instance, whenever they make a den in their garden at home, they don't just hang a blanket over a branch like I do, they build a proper shelter out of sticks and planks of wood and leaves and bits of moss and their parents let them sleep in it – even when it's freezing cold outside. Once they made their own fire and cooked sausages on it WITHOUT A GROWN-UP.

When I heard about this, I invited Isabelle and Alexander Bennett (who are twins in my class at school) to help me make a fire in our garden. But even though the Bennett twins are REALLY good at outdoorsy things, e.g. building dens and climbing trees, and even though they are ALMOST as clever as Tom and Pip,

the fire wouldn't light because all the sticks in my garden were too wet – and then we ran out of matches, so we went inside and made hot chocolate in the microwave instead.

I asked Isabelle and Alexander if they thought we were lacking in the initiative department but Isabelle said not necessarily because initiative is different depending on where you live. Alexander pointed out that some people who live in the countryside and are used to cows and tractors don't have much initiative when it comes to, say, London. And I knew exactly what they meant because when Tom and Pip come to stay with us in our flat they are always stepping off the pavement and nearly getting run over by the Number 73 bus. Last time they came to stay with me they didn't even know about having to wait for their turn at the skate park.

But you don't have to be a genius to know that making a fire needs more initiative than walking along a pavement without getting run over. If my cousins

lived in London, they would learn how to walk to the park and wait for buses in a jiffy.

One day I would like to live with my cousins because life is more fun when they are around to keep me company. Sometimes I ask Mum if we can move to Wales to live next door to them but she says it isn't possible because her job is in London and so is her favourite Turkish restaurant (there are lots of Turkish restaurants near to where we live which is lucky because me, Mum and my big sister Bella (who is at university) love kebabs more than McDonalds).

This is quite a long story because a lot happened at Granny's over the Easter holiday but I will try to give you a shortish version so you won't get bored. Also my hand gets achey if I write for too long.

Tom's hand never gets achey when he writes but that's because he has a new green fountain pen with a padded cushion for his fingers. Plus, he is a brainbox. But Tom didn't fancy writing this book because he has quite a few books of his own to be getting on with, including one about the life cycle of an ant (Tom is going to be a scientist when he grows up, or maybe a jockey).

My cousin Pip didn't want to write it either because you have to sit down to write a book and Pip is not keen on sitting still for longer than a millisecond. She prefers doing cartwheels and climbing trees and she is better at making films than writing.

So that's why you've got me, Joe Robinson, age ten and a quarter. I'll try to make this story gripping and funny all the way to the end and I promise it is a hundred per cent true.

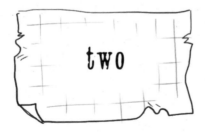

two

I t all started on the second day of our holiday at Granny's when Mr Hodge came round with a pile of leaflets. Mr Hodge is very old and his favourite word is 'fascinating', even though he is not one bit fascinating himself. He has straggly white hair that smells of old sofas and he always wears the same blue jumper with dried soup on it.

Mr Hodge doesn't go anywhere without his metal detector because he is interested in finding 'fascinating' objects that used to belong to people a long time ago, e.g. the Romans. He is also very interested in telling us about the 'fascinating' objects he finds. Once he invited us over to his house in Church Lane to look at a display of Roman artefacts in his living room and even though we stayed for fifty-seven minutes he didn't offer us a biscuit, not even a rich tea.

Now, whenever we see Mr Hodge, we try to make sure we have something important to do so we won't get stuck talking to him.

We were in the sitting room trying to fix a broken video camera that Pip had bought for 99p in a charity shop in Cardiff when we spotted Mr Hodge walking up to Granny's front door. Straight away we grabbed the video camera and tried to escape into the garden before Mr Hodge could see us.

But just as we were running through the hall, Granny answered the front door and suddenly Mr Hodge was inside.

'Oh, there you are, children,' said Granny. 'Mr Hodge has popped over for a cup of tea!'

Tom waved at Mr Hodge and I said 'Hello', but Pip carried on running because she is allergic to making conversation.

Mr Hodge handed Granny a box of chocolates.

'Gosh!' said Granny. 'What have I done to deserve these?'

'Well,' said Mr Hodge, pulling a pile of paper out of his shopping bag. 'Mrs Rooney was selling them at half price! Also I was hoping you might be able to help me fold these leaflets. They're for the parish council meeting this evening.'

Granny looked at her watch.

'Oh, all right!' she said cheerfully. 'You've come to the right house. I have lots of helpers here.'

'Well,' said Mr Hodge, 'I did wonder.'

Me and Tom had to think on our feet because we knew that Granny and Mr Hodge were about to ask us to fold leaflets and one thing I know for a fact is that folding is not quick because once I tried to make a true-life book to get a Blue Peter badge and it took me ALL weekend.

'Oooh, Pip's fallen over!' I said (because Pip was pretending to be hurt in the garden).

'Oh dear, what now!' said Granny, turning round.

'Don't worry, Granny!' shouted Tom, pushing past Granny and Mr Hodge. 'We'll sort Pip out, you just get on with helping Mr Hodge with those leaflets!'

Tom flung open the French doors and grabbed my arm. 'Run!' he said under his breath and we raced out onto the patio.

'Honestly,' said Granny, in a loud voice. 'Those children are a complete menace. They only arrived yesterday and the place is already a bomb site.' I could tell she wasn't really cross, though because when I looked back through the French doors, she gave me a wink.

We pretended to help Pip up and then we decided to play the Boredom Cup in the magnolia tree at the bottom of Granny's garden. The Boredom Cup is one of our favourite games. We play it a lot, even when there are other things we could be doing, e.g. going to the zip wire at the village playground.

The rules of the Boredom Cup are very easy to remember. You just climb a tree and find a good

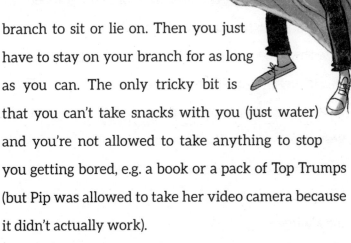

branch to sit or lie on. Then you just have to stay on your branch for as long as you can. The only tricky bit is that you can't take snacks with you (just water) and you're not allowed to take anything to stop you getting bored, e.g. a book or a pack of Top Trumps (but Pip was allowed to take her video camera because it didn't actually work).

The Boredom Cup is more fun than it sounds. Tom invented it and he normally wins because he isn't as fidgety as me and Pip. Plus, he is good at testing himself on capital cities to pass the time. Tom and Pip know more capital cities than I do because their dad (my Uncle Marcus) tests them on long car journeys. Once I asked Mum why she doesn't test me in the car but she said she doesn't have enough headspace to drive AND think of capital cities at the same time. When me and Mum are in the car together we listen to Radio 1.

We had only been playing the Boredom Cup for about ten minutes when Pip, who was on a branch above me, shouted, 'What's that?' and pointed to something in Jeffrey's Meadow.

Tom swung round so fast to look, he nearly off his branch.

'Do you mean the white thing that isn't a cow?' he said.

'It's a sign,' said Pip.

Tom squinted. 'Of what?'

'No,' said Pip. 'An actual sign. Look.'

I pushed a big branch to one side and leaned over so I could see what they were talking about. Right in the middle of Jeffrey's Meadow was a large white noticeboard covered in blue writing, except I couldn't read the writing because it was too small and I don't have supersonic vision, unlike my teacher,

Mr Saunders, who can see EVERYTHING, even when he's on the other side of the classroom.

'Right,' said Tom, wiping his glasses. 'Let's pause the Boredom Cup and go and investigate.'

Tom jumped off his branch and me and Pip climbed down after him because when it comes to investigating in Muddlemoor, there is no time to waste.

Tom and Pip headed over the fence into Jeffrey's Meadow and set off across the damp grass. I tried my best to keep up with them but they had grown a lot since I last saw them and my legs weren't as long.

There weren't any cows, so we didn't need to stick to the edge like we normally do but we still kept our wits about us because once we were chased by a herd of bullocks in Jeffrey's Meadow and Tom says we can never be too careful.

'Do you think it's a poster advertising a circus?' asked Pip. (Pip is mad about circuses and is always hoping one will come to Muddlemoor when we are staying with Granny.)

'I don't think so,' said Tom. 'Jeffrey's Meadow belongs to Mr Draper and I can't imagine that circuses are top of his agenda.'

We nodded because Mr Draper is a local farmer and he is not a pleasant man. Once, when we were picking blackberries near his farmhouse, he set his dog on us and another time, when the vicar was collecting food for the harvest festival, Mr Draper REFUSED to give anything because he said he was 'stone broke' but we knew this wasn't true because he had just bought himself a brand-new Land Rover Discovery.

Mr Draper has a bald head with strands of greasy hair and a long black moustache. He normally drives a tractor or strides around the countryside with a stick but sometimes he sits at a table outside the Old Boot pub and shouts at people. Last summer when Mr Draper was behind Pip in the queue at the village shop he got really impatient because Pip was taking ages to choose her sweets and then he STORMED OUT without paying for his Snickers bar.

When we finally reached the white sign, none of us said anything because we had to concentrate on reading. This is what it said:

ADVANCE WARNING OF PLANNED BUILDING WORKS.

APPLICANT: Mr Fergal Draper

Mr Fergal Draper of Stream Farm, Muddlemoor, has applied for Planning Permission to build an intensive chicken farm on Jeffrey's Meadow in Muddlemoor. The site will comprise of a 20m x 30m chicken enclosure. The enclosure will house between 1,000 and 2,000 chickens (regulations apply).

The PROPOSED CHICKEN FARM will be discussed at the parish council meeting at Muddlemoor Village Hall on 31st March at 5 p.m.

Please submit any questions and objections in writing to the chair of the parish council, Anthea Simmonds.

Tom looked at me and Pip and rubbed his chin.

'Today is the thirty-first of March. This must be the meeting Granny and Mr Hodge are going to later.'

'What do you reck?' said a loud, confident voice.

We spun round and straight away Tom went bright red because it was Sophie Pearce and he has a secret crush on her (except it isn't very secret because everyone knows about it).

'I didn't know you lot were back in Muddlemoor,' she said. 'I'm guessing you've read about the chicken farm.'

We nodded.

'Mr Draper is an EVIL person,' said Sophie. 'He needs to be stopped before he turns this field into a torture chamber.'

'Torture chamber?' I asked, because I couldn't remember reading anything about torturing.

Sophie sighed.

'Torture chamber, battery chicken farm, same difference.' She paused and took a deep breath. 'He's going to pack thousands of chickens into tiny cages and he won't care how they feel because he's only interested in selling cheap eggs to supermarkets and making lots of money. But I know the truth about what goes on behind the scenes and it isn't pretty. Look!'

Sophie held up a magazine with an article about battery chicken farming. One of the photographs was of a chicken trapped in a tiny cage. It didn't look happy.

'Chickens don't deserve this,' said Sophie, tapping the magazine. 'They're lovely creatures, friendly, funny, clever, if you know what you're looking for. I know a lot more about chickens than Fergal Draper and that's why I'm starting a protest group.'

Sophie unrolled a large piece of laminated cardboard, covered in bubble writing. On one side it said:

SAY NO TO BATTERY FARMING!

And on the other it said:

LONG LIVE CHICKENS!

'I'm sticking it OVER this sign,' explained Sophie. 'When you're part of a protest, you don't stop at *anything*.'

Sophie pulled out a roll of black tape and started to stick her poster on top of the white sign.

I waited for Tom to say something but he was a bit too busy staring at his feet.

'Can anyone join your protest group?' I asked, because I couldn't stop thinking about chickens being trapped in tiny cages.

'Course,' said Sophie. 'Make yourselves a placard and come to the village hall later. The parish council are having a meeting about the chicken farm at five and I'm going there to make a loud fuss. I've tipped off the local newspaper.'

Sophie's phone rang.

'Gotta go,' she said, and then she answered her phone and walked back towards the village, talking loudly.

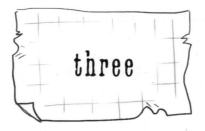

three

As soon as Sophie was out of sight, Tom said that we should make our own placard and join her protest group.

I pointed out that making a placard had actually been MY idea, but I don't think Tom heard me because he said, 'Sophie Pearce has got her head screwed on the right way,' and then he set off across Jeffrey's Meadow at top speed.

Me and Pip ran to keep up, and when we got back to the house Granny and Mr Hodge were *still* folding leaflets in the kitchen. Next to them was the box of chocolates that Mr Hodge had given Granny, except it was open and there weren't any chocolates left. I was a bit disappointed about this because I love all chocolates, even the coffee-flavoured ones that no one else eats.

Mr Hodge shook our hands. His skin felt cool and crumpled, like an old paper bag that has been in a cupboard for a long time. He asked what we had been playing, so I started telling him about the Boredom Cup but before I had finished he said 'Fascinating,' and changed the subject.

'Talking of which,' he said, 'I've just been telling your grandmother about my latest discovery. I found a fragment of an old Roman spoon in Stonely Park. I bet you have no idea what spoons like that were used for?'

'Eating?' said Tom, who is always keen on knowing the right answer, even when Mr Hodge is asking the questions. 'Taking medicine? Stirring coffee?'

'Excellent suggestions!' said Mr Hodge, chuckling. 'And, yes, you'd think a spoon would have a practical use, wouldn't you, but it's rather more interesting than that.' Mr Hodge laughed excitedly and cleared his throat. 'This type of spoon was too decorative for eating, it was given as a gift at Roman christenings. Isn't that fascinating?'

Mr Hodge looked at us with big eyes and waited for us to answer but we didn't have anything to say because old spoons are not fascinating to everybody, e.g. us.

Granny burst out laughing.

'Don't take it personally, Anthony,' she said, refilling their cups of tea. 'One thing we CAN be sure of is that these three have something more pressing to do than talk to us about fascinating old spoons. Am I right, children?'

I looked at the clock and explained that we only had one hour left before the parish council meeting at the village hall.

'Why on earth are you so interested in the parish council meeting?' asked Granny.

I tried really hard to think of a good fib but I couldn't think of one so I ended up spilling the beans.

I told Granny and Mr Hodge about the sign in the middle of Jeffrey's Meadow and about the picture of the chickens trapped in tiny cages and finally I mentioned Sophie Pearce's protest group.

'So that's why we want to make a protest placard of our own.'

I was slightly worried that Granny might be cross because not everybody is keen on protests in case they

lead to riots but luckily Granny said, 'Good for you.'
Then she told us that when she was younger she used
to go on lots of protest marches with her friends.

'Once, we camped by a river for three months to
protest against a new motorway but then we got flooded
out and had to be rescued by a police speedboat.'

Mr Hodge looked impressed. 'Jenny!' he said (because
Jenny is Granny's real name), and then he cleared his
throat and started telling us about Roman protests. 'Do
you want to hear about Reminulus, a famous Roman
protestor? It's a fascinating story.'

'Perhaps later, Anthony,' said Granny kindly.

She explained that various people in Muddlemoor
weren't keen on the chicken farm either and that was
why the parish council was holding a meeting later, to
discuss the proposal.

'Some of us have signed a petition and Anthea
has written these leaflets,' she explained. 'But it's
going to take a lot of determination to vote against
him. Landowners like Mr Draper have a lot of power.

He's been promising members of the parish council a lifetime's supply of free eggs if they vote in favour of his chicken farm. Some of the members who live in Cudlington are pretty tempted by that, and I can't say I blame them.'

'But chicken farms are torture chambers,' I pointed out.

'Now, come on you lot. Mr Draper wouldn't deliberately torture animals,' said Granny. 'He's a pretty respected farmer, has been for years. He's always looked after his cows impeccably. My guess is, he needs the money and that's why he's so keen on branching into chicken farming. He's not actually going to HARM the chickens.'

'Still cruel to keep them in tiny cages, though,' I said, and Granny ruffled my hair.

We left Granny and Mr Hodge folding leaflets and got started on our placards. I drew one with a big picture of a chicken (except it looked more like a dinosaur because I'm not brilliant at art even though it is my favourite subject).

'Sorry it's not a very good drawing,' I said, but Pip told me it wasn't THAT bad and Tom pointed out that protest placards did not have to be ARTISTIC, they just had to be bright and dramatic.

That's the nice thing about cousins. They make you feel better about the things you feel rubbish about, which is the exact opposite of most people at my school, e.g. Dylan Moynihan.

Tom painted the chicken in bright orange and red and Pip wrote *SAVE ME!* in red paint because she is good at bubble writing. Then we made a few more.

We showed the placards to Granny and Mr Hodge, who were in the hallway putting on their coats.

Mr Hodge said, 'Fascinating,' and Granny smiled and said, 'Well, they will certainly stand out in a crowd.'

'But remember,' she said, going a bit serious, 'it may not be possible to stop Mr Draper. He might have every right to build a chicken shed on his own land and

he isn't going to appreciate being told what to do by what he calls "the piddling parish council" or, for that matter, by three interfering children who don't even live here. Promise me you won't do anything silly?'

We nodded because Granny's eyes had gone all serious but we crossed our fingers behind our backs because that is a cunning thing to do if you need to make a promise that might be quite tricky to keep.

Except I can't get away with this tactic at home because my mum always knows when my fingers are crossed behind my back, even if I hide them under the sleeves of my jumper. Once I asked Mum if she had x-ray vision and she said, 'I have superpower eyes, I can see what you're up to even when I'm asleep.' I asked Mum if seeing in your sleep was quite a rare talent and she laughed and said, 'Not for mums, it isn't.'

'Come on,' said Granny. 'Let's get this meeting over and done with so we can get back in time for *Cul-de-Sac*.' *Cul-de-Sac* is Granny's favourite TV show. It's really good.

We set off down Little Draycott. On the way we bumped into some of Granny's neighbours: Bob and Sally Merry and their giant poodle Puff. Straight away Puff jumped up and knocked me over but I didn't mind because I am mad about dogs, even naughty ones. Sally and Bob kept apologising and saying that Puff was normally really well behaved and I didn't know what to say because Puff is the naughtiest dog I know and her favourite thing is jumping up and knocking people over.

Ronnie Mehta was talking on his phone in his front garden. He waved at us and smiled and we smiled back because we really like Ronnie Mehta and we quite like his teenage daughters, when they're not stealing our biscuits.

At the end of Little Draycott, just before we reached the main road, we bumped into Granny's friend Anthea. She was carrying a clipboard, a notebook and a big box of chocolates and she was rushing because she is the chair of the parish council

and didn't want to be late for the meeting.

She saluted when she saw us. 'I see that your trusty bodyguards are back in town!' she said to Granny.

'Oh yes,' said Granny. 'Which means nothing can possibly go wrong for the next few weeks.'

Anthea and Granny laughed really loudly.

'Good heavens, what do they feed you in Wales?' she said to Tom and Pip. 'You're enormous!' and then she looked at me and said, 'Hello, young Joey.'

I did not smile because for one thing I hate being called Joey, for another thing, I am not keen on Anthea (although I am quite fond of her cats; she has seven) and for an extra thing, I'm fed up with not growing.

Anthea spotted our protest placards.

'Good stuff. Our cause could do with some young blood.'

'Anthea is an excellent chair,' Granny said. 'If anyone can stop Mr Draper's chicken farm, it's her.'

Anthea snorted. 'Nonsense. Team effort, that's what we need. The three Ps – People. Pressure.

Perseverance. Fifty pence to the first person who can spell Perseverance?'

I did not say anything because when it comes to spelling, my brain is not one hundred per cent reliable.

'P-E-R-S-A...' began Tom.

'Wrong!' shouted Anthea, roaring with laughter. 'Good grief, what do they teach you at school these days? Look it up in a dictionary and I'll test you again tomorrow. Come on, everyone, time is of the essence. Someone needs to teach Fergal Draper about democracy. Democracy – there's another word for you to learn, children!'

For some reason Anthea loves testing us on things we don't know and she always seems to know what we are up to, even when it is top secret. Tom says it's because she used to be a spy but I think it's because she is nosy. Even though Anthea is Granny's friend we don't enjoy having to improve our education in the school holidays.

The main road through Muddlemoor was busier

than usual because people were heading to the parish council meeting. It was a sunny day and the blossom on the trees smelled like Fruit Pastilles. A bit of me wished that we were off to play the Boredom Cup again instead of going to a protest, but I kept quiet about this because I wasn't sure if Tom and Pip would agree. They don't get as excited as I do about climbing trees because in Wales they have a woodland next to their house and they can go in it whenever they like as long as they have done their homework.

'Ban battery farms! Chickens have rights! Ban battery farms! Chickens have rights!'

Sophie Pearce was standing outside the village hall and she

was shouting loudly.

'Thanks for coming, guys,' she said breathlessly as we joined her on the steps. 'Make a bit of noise, will you. If we cause a riot, the press might show up.'

Granny agreed that we could stay outside protesting with Sophie while she went to the meeting.

'Wait for me on the steps after the meeting,' she said, 'and we'll walk home together. I won't be more than half an hour.'

We waited for Granny and Anthea to go into the hall and then we started shouting 'Save our Chickens!' at the tops of our voices but just as I was shouting 'Ch–', Mr Draper walked past. He was carrying a large tray of cupcakes and pulling on the lead of a snarling dog.

'Rufus doesn't like people shouting,' he said nastily.

'Especially children. He'll bite you if you keep up that racket.'

Rufus barked and

straight away Tom stopped shouting because although he is mostly brave he doesn't like risking serious injuries, e.g. dog bites. A few seconds later, me and Pip stopped too because Rufus's teeth looked really sharp.

But Sophie Pearce wasn't scared of Rufus or Mr Draper. 'Chicken murderer!' she shouted even more loudly and then she pointed out that it would take more than a tray of homemade cakes to get the parish council to vote for him.

Mr Draper laughed nastily. 'Let's see about that, shall we, princess. Anyway, I'm a farmer, not a murderer. Animal welfare is top of the agenda.'

Sophie scowled. 'Animal welfare doesn't mean keeping chickens in tiny cages.'

'Tiny?' said Mr Draper. 'Have you seen the size of the cages I'm proposing? Those chickens are going to have plenty of space to skip around in, don't you worry your pretty little head.'

Sophie scowled. 'You COULD turn Jeffrey's Meadow into a free-range farm where chickens can walk freely and have a nice life.'

'I could, princess, but it's all about margins these days. The wife wants a time-share in Malta.'

Sophie scowled.

'Don't call me *princess*,' she said.

Mr Draper yanked on Rufus's lead and laughed.

'No problem, chick. See you later, I'm off to put an end to the ageing parish council.'

He walked up the steps and disappeared into the village hall.

Sophie threw down her placard.

'Idiot!' she said crossly. 'He's right, though. The parish council is just a bunch of small-town OAPs with too much time on their hands. How ARE they going to stop a man like Mr Draper?'

I thought of the pictures of the trapped chickens and I thought of Jeffrey's Meadow being covered in a large chicken barn. I held my placard high above my head and shouted, 'Ban battery farms', as loudly as I could.

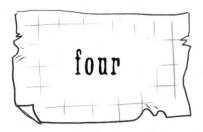

four

The problem about protesting is that it is only fun for about five minutes.

Even shouting is boring after a while (especially if there is nobody to hear you) and it SLIGHTLY hurts your throat. Plus, holding placards up in the air is more tiring than you think.

After about ten minutes we stopped for a rest.

Tom started sharpening a pencil with a stone and Pip pretended to film him with her video camera.

'You making a film?' asked Sophie, spotting the video camera. 'Cool.'

Pip chewed her lip. 'Um, it doesn't work,' she said. I could tell that Pip was a bit embarrassed to be caught playing with a broken camera.

'Shame. We could have filmed a protest video and sent it to the local TV news station. If they won't come to us, we need to go to them.'

'Can't we film a protest video on your phone?' I asked.

'Nah, the camera's broken. I'm saving up for a new one.'

Shouting came from inside the village hall. Tom stopped sharpening his pencil and looked up.

'Do you think something bad is happening in there?' I asked.

'Doubt it,' said Sophie. 'I reckon it's just a heated debate. Listen, you can hear Mr Draper interrupting everybody like he is the blinking mayor or something.'

The shouting got louder and I started breathing really loudly because that is what I do when I think something bad is going to happen. Like for instance, once I started breathing very loudly in a maths test because I had forgotten to revise and I couldn't answer one single question and Miss Perkins sent me to the school nurse and I missed the test. Except when it

happened the next day in a spelling test, Miss Perkins told me to stay in my seat and ever since then she hasn't taken my loud breathing seriously.

'You got asthma or something?' said Sophie, not looking up because she was busy texting.

'Erm,' I said, because I have never in my life suffered from asthma even though I would quite like to have a blue and white inhaler like Trixie Sargeant. 'I'm just a bit worried that Mr Draper is torturing the parish council to make them vote for his chicken farm. Didn't you hear what he said about "putting an end" to them?'

Tom looked up.

'That's what dictators do,' he said. 'We've been studying it in history at school. If voting doesn't go their way, dictators get rid of the people who vote against them.'

I didn't like the sound of Mr Draper getting rid of Granny. For one thing, what would happen to us? We would probably be able to cook ourselves dinner if we stuck to something simple, e.g. toast and Marmite, but

I was a bit worried about locking the house at night because I'm not sure where Granny keeps her spare keys. I was also slightly worried about money because we had spent all our pocket money on sweets at the village shop yesterday and we didn't have any left for food, not even one pence.

Sophie Pearce laughed. 'Tom,' she said, 'is there anyone you DON'T suspect of being a criminal?'

And straight away Tom went back to sharpening his pencil.

'Do you think we should go inside and rescue Granny?' I asked.

Tom shook his head but I could tell he was just pretending not to be worried because of Sophie Pearce.

I stared at the clock above the door of the village hall. Half an hour had already passed and the meeting hadn't finished. I was beginning to get hungry.

Another twenty minutes went by before we heard chairs scraping across the floor and people saying 'Thank you'. Then the door opened and everybody piled out onto the steps, talking loudly. Nobody looked as if they had been tortured and Granny was eating a cupcake.

'Hello, you lot,' she said. 'Sorry it went on for so long.' She paused and started to whisper. 'Mr Draper had A LOT to say for himself and he doesn't like being interrupted. He brought along some new drawings for this wretched chicken barn and has now managed to delay the vote until Monday to give everyone the chance to have a look at the new plans. He gave everyone homemade cakes *and* he's promised us all a gallon of free milk fresh from the farm on Saturday morning.' Granny rolled her eyes and grinned at us. 'To soften us all up, no doubt. Although I must say, those cupcakes were absolutely delicious!'

'Ooh,' said Tom, perking up. 'Are there any left?'

'I'm afraid not, they went in a jiffy.' Granny paused. 'Anthea had two! But if Mr Draper thinks a few cakes are going to make some of us change our minds about his horrible chicken farm . . . well, then he is horribly mistaken.'

At that moment Mr Draper walked past, carrying an empty tray and yanking on Rufus's lead.

'See you all for your free milk on Saturday,' he said, smiling nastily at Granny, Anthea and Mr Hodge (the Merrys had already left because they were late for Puff's dinner). 'And don't say I don't do anything for the good people of Muddlemoor.'

On the way back, Granny and Anthea discussed the meeting.

'He holds all the cards,' said Granny.

'Nonsense,' replied Anthea. 'He can't start building until he has consent from the parish council. And that means US. So long as we vote against him on

Monday he'll have to delay building work and take his case to the county council in Stonely. He'll be livid if he has to do that.'

Granny nodded. 'Yes, but some members of the council are ready to let him go ahead – did you hear what Louise Fletton said? She doesn't want to fall out with Draper in case he bans people from walking on his fields. And Mrs Rooney doesn't want to risk losing a valued customer. The voters from Cudlington can't think of anything beyond the lifetime of free eggs he has promised them. What with eggs and cakes and free milk, Fergal Draper has this bribery business sewn up.'

Anthea snorted. 'Then we have to stand up to bribery. No one has any backbone these days, that's the problem.'

Granny asked Anthea if she wanted to come in for a cup of tea but Anthea said she had a bit of a stomach ache and was going to lie down. 'Which is a shame, because I was looking forward to catching up with the Terrible Trio,' she said, nodding at us. 'No doubt they are up to SOMETHING they shouldn't be.'

She clutched her stomach.

'Gosh, I really shouldn't have eaten all that cake.'

'Poor you,' said Granny kindly. 'Come to think of it, I don't feel a hundred per cent myself.'

'Perhaps we're allergic to Fergal Draper!'

Anthea and Granny started laughing but then they had to stop because Anthea thought she might actually BE sick and then she raced into her house without saying goodbye.

'Very unlike Anthea to be off-colour,' said Granny and even though she was trying to smile I couldn't help noticing that her skin had turned ever so slightly green.

'It's been a long afternoon and I think we could all do with a spot of *Cul-de-Sac*,' she said weakly.

But when we got home, Granny didn't even watch *Cul-de-Sac* with us. She spent AGES in the loo and then she went for a lie down in her bedroom.

'I'm so sorry,' she said, when we went upstairs to check on her. 'Do you think you could manage to make yourselves something to eat? I must have caught Anthea's sick bug.'

So we ate Marmite on toast in front of *Jaws* and after that we didn't feel like eating a proper dinner (because shark attacks slightly put you off your food) so we went upstairs to say good night to Granny and headed to bed ourselves.

We stayed up for ages talking because it felt a bit strange being awake when Granny was fast asleep. I asked Tom and Pip how long they thought Granny would be ill for and Pip said that once Tom had caught a sick bug on Christmas Eve and even though he puked five times, he was fine again by Christmas Day.

'That's true,' agreed Tom. 'I still managed to eat a whole chocolate Santa and two sugar mice at six a.m.

on Christmas morning.'

And Pip nodded.

'In that case, Granny should be fine again by breakfast,' I said. I was glad about this, partly because I was worried about Granny but mainly because Granny had promised to take us to the adventure playground. I put my head down on my pillow and thought of all the different things at the adventure playground, e.g. a rope bridge that went over a REAL moat and a drawbridge that went up and down.

But just as I was falling asleep, Tom started talking about Sophie Pearce again.

'We need to do more to help her cause,' he said.

'Shall we make another protest placard?' I suggested, because I quite fancied having another go at drawing a chicken.

Tom shook his head. 'Remember what she said about making a protest film? THAT'S what we need to do.' He paused. 'Pip, where's your camera?'

Pip looked worried.

'Why?'

'I'm going to try to fix it.'

Pip gulped and I could tell she wasn't keen on letting Tom fix her video camera because once when Tom tried to fix Pip's alarm clock, he took the whole thing apart and then he couldn't put it back together again and Pip had to throw the alarm clock in the bin (except she ended up taking it out of the bin afterwards because one thing about Pip is that she doesn't like throwing things away, even when they're broken).

Pip clutched the video camera to her chest.

'Pip!' said Tom, all impatient. 'It's our only chance to help Sophie Pearce's good cause.' He stopped being impatient and looked sad. 'Think of all those chickens, spending their lives in tiny cages.'

Pip had a long think and eventually she pulled the

video camera out from underneath her and nodded.

Tom grinned.

'Right,' he said, 'I'm going to find a screwdriver.'

While Tom rummaged around in his army rucksack, I went over to Pip's bed to have a look at the camera. I tried to remember what Mum had done when she fixed the TV remote control, except I couldn't remember much because I don't think I had been listening very hard at the time. But then all of a sudden it didn't matter that I couldn't remember how to fix a remote control because at that exact moment I spotted a hidden compartment on the video camera. Its catch was really worn out but when I looked closely I could see that it said *Batteries*.

Tom came over and took the camera from Pip. He started to unscrew the back cover.

'Wait!' I said, all excited. 'I don't think it needs fixing, it just needs new batteries. Look!'

I took the camera from Tom and pointed to the battery compartment. 'Double As! Granny's got loads of those, we can ask her where she keeps them in the morning.'

Tom and Pip stared at the battery compartment and I could tell they were pleased because Pip said, 'Well spotted, Joe,' and Tom got out his green fountain pen and started writing.

Muddlemoor Productions presents

The Chicken Farm Protest Film

Reporter: * Sophie Pearce *

Writer, director, producer: Tom Berryman

Camerawoman: Pip Berryman

Back-up operations: Joe Robinson

And even though I wasn't sure what 'back-up operations' meant, I knew that Tom was serious about the film because Sophie Pearce's name was surrounded by tiny green stars.

five

One thing that makes grown-ups REALLY grumpy is being woken up when they are fast asleep.

Sometimes I can't help waking Mum up if I have a bad dream and she is fine with this because bad dreams count as an emergency. But lots of middle-of-the-night things DON'T count as emergencies, e.g.:

Being thirsty

Being hungry

Being hot

Being cold

Being bored

Being excited

Being itchy

Being keen to make flapjacks for the school cake sale

Another thing that doesn't count as an emergency is 'needing to find batteries'.

I know this for a fact because the morning after the parish council meeting we woke up REALLY early, i.e. before 6 a.m., and the first thing we thought about was fixing Pip's video camera. Except we couldn't find batteries ANYWHERE in Granny's house so we went upstairs to wake Granny.

Tom said 'Granny!' in a normalish loud whisper but she didn't move a muscle, not even an eyelash, so I tapped her on the shoulder and said 'Granny!' in a much louder voice – and that worked.

When Granny spotted me staring into her eyes, she started screaming. Her hair was all sticky-uppy and she looked a bit like a zombie. 'What on earth is going on?' she said, all squeaky.

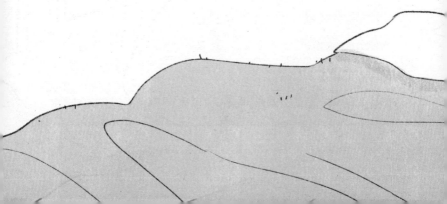

Tom cleared his throat. 'I'm afraid it's an emergency, Granny. We need batteries!'

Granny looked at us for a long time without speaking.

Eventually she said, 'Hmmmm,' and then she said it a bit louder and finally she said, 'Why do I smell a rat?' and at that point I jumped on to her bed because even though rats are living creatures (and I love ALL living

creatures), I can't help jumping on to beds when I hear about one.

'I can't smell anything,' said Tom vaguely and Pip stared at the ceiling because when it is 5.55 a.m. she is even quieter than normal.

'You know perfectly well that "smelling a rat" is an expression,' said Granny, sounding MUCH crosser than usual. 'And in answer to your question, the battery box is in the top drawer of the dresser in the kitchen but just so you know for next time: needing to find batteries is NOT AN EMERGENCY!'

I said 'Sorry,' because saying sorry is always a sensible thing to do when grown-ups are cross and then I said, 'Are you feeling better, Granny?' because I was still genuinely worried about Granny's health.

Granny sighed. 'Well, I don't feel a hundred per cent but this MAY have SOMETHING to do with being woken up when I was having a lovely dream about swimming in the Bahamas.'

I gave Granny a hug and said sorry again and then

we tiptoed downstairs to find the battery box.

It was exactly where Granny said it would be, i.e. in the top drawer of the dresser in the kitchen. We rummaged around until we found two batteries that said AA on them. Pip forced open the battery compartment of the camera and popped the batteries in. She pressed the power button but nothing happened so then she took the batteries out again, switched them around and tried the power button again. This time a green light came on.

Pip pressed the record button and the camera started whirring. She looked through the lens and filmed me and Tom for a minute and when she played it back we could see and hear us PERFECTLY on the playback screen.

Pip grinned and I laughed and Tom said, 'Bingo!' and we were all flabbergasted because we are not normally successful when it comes to fixing things.

After that we ate breakfast and I made Granny a cup of tea because I am used to doing that for Mum when

she feels poorly. Granny said 'Thank you,' and she also said that she was going to stay in bed for the morning but we could go into the village if we wanted to as long as we put away our cereal bowls and cleaned our teeth and came back for lunch.

So we did all the things she'd told us to do (except I might have accidentally forgotten to clean my teeth) and then we went to look for Sophie Pearce because we wanted to tell her that we had fixed the camera and could help her make a protest film if she still wanted to. First of all, we went to her house on Church Lane but her dad said she was feeding some chickens in Golders Close, so then we went to the Flettons' because they live in Golders Close and they have chickens but Sophie wasn't there either. We checked at the church because the vicar has a chicken run in his front garden but she wasn't there and finally we went to the shop.

Mrs Rooney was stacking boxes outside her shop.

'Do you think I'm a lost and found office or

something?' said Mrs Rooney.

And we said, 'No.'

'Well then, buy something or bizzle off,' she said crossly and we had to go because we didn't have any money to buy anything, not even one pence.

Luckily, when we got back to Granny's, we spotted Sophie Pearce at the far end of Little Draycott (which is the name of Granny's lane). We ran all the way to the bottom of Little Draycott and eventually we caught up with her. She was nailing posters to a closed gate that led directly on to Mr Draper's farmyard.

'Sophie!' I shouted when we got close. 'We've been looking for you everyw—'

'*Shhhhhhh!*' she said, spinning round. 'Mr Draper caught me putting these up earlier and pulled them all down, so I'm trying to keep a low profile.'

Tom flicked his hair. 'We fixed Pip's camera.'

'Oh!' Sophie grinned. 'Nice one.'

I asked Sophie if she still wanted us to film her making a protest video and she said 'Sure.'

So Tom showed Sophie his notes about the protest film and Sophie said 'Awesome', and then Tom hid behind Pip so nobody would notice him blushing (except me and Pip both noticed because it's hard not to notice when someone's cheeks turn the same colour as strawberry jelly).

Sophie suggested we film her in front of Mr Draper's gate 'to give the film context', and I nodded even though I didn't know what 'context' meant. She leaned against the gate and Pip pressed the record button, then Sophie started talking all about Mr Draper and his chicken farm. It took ages because Tom kept saying 'Cut' and 'Take twenty-seven' and acting like he was a professional film director.

After a while Sophie said, 'I'm actually in a bit of a hurry, Tom. Got chickens to feed,' and then Tom stopped speaking and Pip finished the film in a jiffy.

It was a good thing we had finished filming because at that moment Mr Draper stomped across the farmyard.

'Get 'em, Rufus!' he laughed, as his dog Rufus ran straight towards us. 'Bring 'em down!'

Rufus leaped over the gate, knocked Tom to the ground and stood on top of him, barking.

For a few seconds everything went still. I thought of the time Ivan Ashby who lives on our street in London got attacked by an out-of-control doberman. It happened just outside our flat so Mum called an ambulance and later that day Ivan Ashby came over to give Mum a bunch of flowers as a thank you present and he had thirty-six stitches.

'Rufus!' I called nervously.

Rufus didn't move.

I found half a biscuit in my pocket and held it in my

outstretched hand.

Rufus still didn't move.

Mr Draper opened the gate and stomped over.

'Drop!' he shouted at Rufus. 'Drop!'

Rufus ignored him.

'Mercy!' screamed Tom. 'Save me! I'm too young to die!'

'Keep calm, Tom,' said Sophie.

But I don't think Sophie realised that Tom can't keep calm when sharp teeth are involved.

'Puff!' came a woman's voice from further up the lane. 'Puff!'

We spun round.

Bob and Sally Merry's dog Puff was running down Little Draycott towards us, closely followed by Sally Merry.

'Heel, Puff! Heel!' called Sally.

As soon as Rufus saw Puff he stopped barking and wagged his tail. He stepped politely off Tom and trotted towards her. The two dogs sniffed each other and Tom leaped to his feet.

'Get that poodle away from my dog,' Mr Draper said nastily. 'She's been coming down to the farm and bothering Rufus for months.'

Sally smiled. 'I'm so sorry, Fergal. Puff's usually SO obedient! I don't know what's got into her. Heel, Puff! Heel!'

Puff wagged her tail and ran off towards the small woodland that lay to the left of Stream Farm. Rufus ran after her.

'Oh, heavens!' said Sally, giggling.

Mr Draper gave her a murderous look.

'Now look what she's done,' he said furiously,

shutting the gate and stomping up the lane, towards the woods.

'And what are you kids doing all the way down here, anyway?' he said, calling over his shoulder. 'If I catch you spying on my farm again I'll be straight on the phone to your grandmother. Go on, scram!'

Sally smiled kindly.

'Off you go, you lot,' she said. 'Head home to Granny and I'll help Fergal track down those naughty doglets.'

Tom brushed dirt off his jeans.

'Are you all right, Tom?' asked Sophie.

'Fine,' Tom muttered. 'I'm not scared of dogs.' But his face had gone the colour of cold porridge and I could tell he was just pretending not to be scared.

Sophie shook her head. 'I told you Fergal Draper is a dangerous man,' she said. 'That's why we need to stop him building this evil chicken shed.' She peered at Pip's camera. 'Can I see if your camera's cable is compatible with my phone?' We watched as Sophie plugged Pip's cable carefully into her phone.

'Cool,' she said eventually. 'It works. Can I upload your video on to my phone, Pip? If it's good enough, I'll send it off to the local TV news this afternoon.'

Pip nodded and we all stood around while the videos uploaded.

'Cheers, guys,' said Sophie when the upload had finished. 'The sooner we get this battery chicken farm on the news, the better.'

Sophie waved goodbye and walked back up Little Draycott, towards the village.

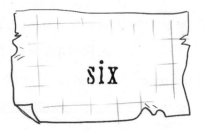

six

By the time we got back to Granny's we were starving (because that's what happens if you run everywhere). Granny was still in her dressing gown but she was on the phone to Anthea, so we helped ourselves to a plate of biscuits and watched the video of Sophie through the playback screen on Pip's camera.

At first we were a bit disappointed because Pip had cut out a lot of Sophie's face and had ended up filming half of Mr Draper's empty farmyard instead but when we watched the film back for a second time, Tom said, 'Did you see that?' And, when me and Pip shook our heads, Tom rewound the video and paused.

'That!' he said.

I stared at the screen and chewed my lip, because apart from Sophie, all I could see was a white delivery van parked in the farmyard in the background.

'Do you see what I see?' said Tom, all spluttery.

Me and Pip stared at the screen.

'I'm not sure,' I said. 'I see a white van.'

Tom turned his head away from Granny and started to whisper.

'It's not just a white van. Look at the black thing on the side.'

Me and Pip moved closer to the playback screen on the video camera and made our eyes go squinty and eventually we saw what Tom was talking about. On the side of the van was . . .

. . . a black skull and crossbones.

Tom stared at me and Pip with his mouth wide open and me and Pip stared back at him because we were still a bit confused.

'Is Mr Draper a pirate?' I asked, because the only time I had ever seen a skull and crossbones was in books about pirates.

'NO!' said Tom, all spluttery. 'In real life, skull and crossbones don't mean pirates. Skull and crossbones mean . . . POISON!'

I squealed so loudly that Granny looked up from her conversation with Anthea.

'What's up?' she said, so I mumbled, 'Nothing,' and she went back to talking to Anthea.

'Oh dear, not Anthony too?' she said down the phone. 'The whole parish council is dropping like flies!'

Granny put down the phone.

'Well,' she said. 'Poor Anthea is still feeling ever so poorly, far worse than me, and Anthony Hodge has been on the toilet all morning. That's half the parish council laid low with this sick bug. At this

rate most of the council will be too ill to vote at Monday's meeting!' She yawned. 'Goodness, is it nearly lunchtime? I've been in bed all morning and completely lost track of time!'

She started getting ham and cucumber out of the fridge. When her back was turned Tom hissed at me and Pip to follow him into the sitting room. When we got there he sat down on the blue velvet armchair and stared at us.

'I think I know why half the parish council are ill,' he said slowly. 'I THINK MR DRAPER POISONED THOSE CUPCAKES.'

I put my hand over my mouth to stop myself from squealing again.

'Are you sure?' I asked, because it was probably the most serious accusation we had EVER made.

Tom took a very long breath. 'I'm positive. Mr Draper is worried the parish council will vote against his chicken shed. So he deliberately delayed the vote until Monday – and then fed them poisoned cupcakes so they won't be well enough to vote.'

Tom went over to Granny's computer and loaded Google and typed in the search box: *Symptoms of poisoning.*

70,777,000 results came up. Tom clicked on the top one:

Signs and symptoms of poisoning

The symptoms of poisoning will depend on the type of poison and the amount taken in, but general things to look out for include:

- drowsiness
- vomiting
- stomach pains
- confusion

Tom quit the browser and copied everything into his notebook.

'Granny has ALL those symptoms. She keeps yawning and wanting to go to bed and she feels sick and she has stomach pains and . . .' Tom paused. 'Just now, she said she was really confused about what time of day it is, didn't she?'

Me and Pip nodded. Straight away I started getting butterflies in my stomach because everything Tom said made sense. I couldn't help wishing that we were still playing the Boredom Cup in the magnolia tree at the bottom of the garden.

'Plus,' continued Tom, 'remember what Anthea said yesterday about eating TWO of Mr Draper's cupcakes? That must be why she's iller than Granny. She had a double dose!' He paused. 'And by the looks of the delivery van parked in his farmyard this morning, he might do it again.'

Tom started writing more things in his notebook and Pip rewatched the film on her video camera.

But I raced back to the kitchen because when you've just been told that an evil farmer has poisoned your grandmother, it is quite important to keep a close eye on her at all times.

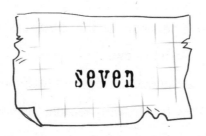

seven

For the whole of that afternoon and for half of the next day we concentrated on staying inside and keeping an eye on Granny because we agreed that it was the safest thing to do in the circumstances. I made her cups of tea and Tom and Pip made Marmite on toast and sometimes we took her an apple for vitamins.

It was quite hard work looking after Granny for hours on end but it was worth it because by lunchtime on Friday she was feeling much better. She made us cheese sandwiches and orange squash for lunch and told us to eat outside in the garden because we'd been inside too long and needed some fresh air.

I was a bit worried about leaving Granny in the house on her own in case Mr Draper came round and tried to poison her again but Tom pointed out that we wouldn't be much use to Granny if we got weak from lack of fresh air so we took our sandwiches over to the weeping willow tree in Ronnie Mehta's garden and ate them while we discussed a plan of action.

Pip said she thought we should go and ask Mr Draper and see how he reacted but Tom shook his head. He said we needed to build a strong case against Mr Draper FIRST because that is what proper detectives do (Tom is more up-to-date on detectives than most people because he reads a lot of detective books. Also, Tom is not as brave as Pip).

At this point Tom and Pip started having an argument. This was quite unusual for them because they don't argue as much as most brothers and sisters.

'The last thing we want,' said Tom, 'is to get our facts wrong, then WE'LL be the ones in trouble and he'll be free to go round poisoning whoever he likes. What we need to do is get a rock-solid case against him. We need to find out if other members of the parish council,

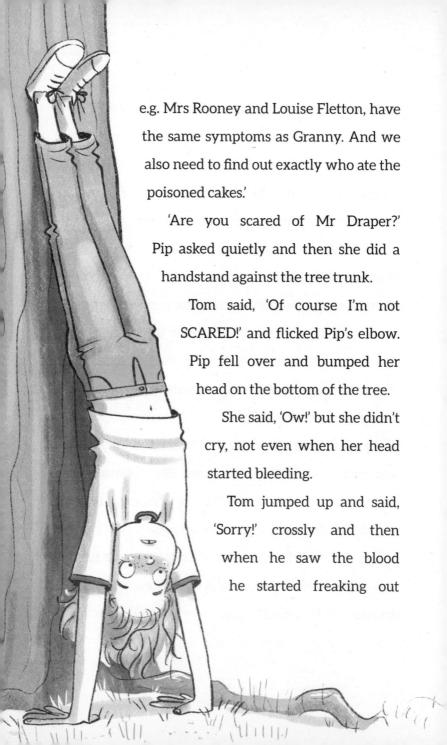

e.g. Mrs Rooney and Louise Fletton, have the same symptoms as Granny. And we also need to find out exactly who ate the poisoned cakes.'

'Are you scared of Mr Draper?' Pip asked quietly and then she did a handstand against the tree trunk.

Tom said, 'Of course I'm not SCARED!' and flicked Pip's elbow. Pip fell over and bumped her head on the bottom of the tree.

She said, 'Ow!' but she didn't cry, not even when her head started bleeding.

Tom jumped up and said, 'Sorry!' crossly and then when he saw the blood he started freaking out and saying 'DO YOU NEED TO GO TO A&E?' in a really panicky voice (because one thing Tom hates is the sight of blood).

But Pip said she definitely didn't need to go to A&E because it was a just a graze.

And then Tom said 'Sorry,' in a much nicer voice and Pip told him it was OK.

Tom announced that he was happy to do what Pip suggested and confront Mr Draper but not until we had built a strong case against him. 'After all,' he said, 'when it comes to accusations, we don't exactly have a very good history.'

Pip said, 'Fine,' and Tom said, 'Good,' and I said, 'Are you sure we shouldn't just warn Granny?' and they both said, 'No,' because when it comes to keeping secrets, they are much better than me.

We started thinking of all the questions we needed to ask the parish council and then Tom wrote them down so we wouldn't forget.

Tom, Pip and Joe's list of questions for Muddlemoor parish council

How many people were at the parish council meeting?

Who ate just one of Mr Draper's cupcakes?

Who ate MORE than one of Mr Draper's cupcakes (not including Anthea because we know that she ate two)?

Who has symptoms of poisoning, e.g. drowsiness, sickness, stomach pains, confusion?

We took our empty plates back to Granny's and she said we could go back out as long as we were back by 4 p.m.

'I'm sorry we still haven't been to the adventure playground,' she said, 'I'll take you as soon as I'm well enough.'

'Don't worry, Granny,' said Tom, patting her on the back. 'You just concentrate on getting better.' And then just as we were walking out of the room he said, 'By the way, Granny, how many people are on the parish council?'

Granny chuckled and said, 'Why on earth do you need to know that?' But she didn't wait for an answer because she was busy counting on her fingers.

'Not many of us, that's for sure. Eleven, I think.' She paused to count again. 'Me, Anthea, Bob and Sally Merry, Louise Fletton, Anthony Hodge, Mrs Rooney – and then four others from Cudlington who I don't know very well. A small but fearsome bunch!'

Tom wrote the names down in his notebook and Pip grabbed her video camera from the kitchen table.

'Bye, Granny,' we shouted and climbed through the hedge into the Merrys' garden.

Sally Merry was hanging up washing.

'Hello again, children! I don't suppose you've seen Puff, have you? She's run off again and it took me AGES to get her back from the woods yesterday.'

We shook our heads.

'Oh dear,' said Sally. 'I'll just finish hanging this up and then I'll go and look for her.'

Tom cleared his throat.

'Are you feeling OK, Tom?' asked Sally.

'Oh, I'M fine,' said Tom in his serious voice. 'But what about YOU? Are YOU feeling OK? Not under the weather?'

Sally laughed.

'I'm tickety-boo. Unlike poor Bob, who has taken to the sofa with a nasty tummy ache.'

Pip elbowed me in the ribs and Tom started updating his notes at top speed.

'Poor Bob,' I said. 'Does he have any other symptoms? Vomiting, confusion, drowsiness?'

Sally raised her eyebrows. 'No, just the tummy ache,' she said, looking at me carefully.

I gulped.

'He was OK when we saw him at the meeting the other night.'

'Yes, he got ill after the meeting. Must have been all

that talk of a chicken farm! Fergal Draper is enough to make anyone feel poorly.'

Sally disappeared behind a bright pink duvet cover and Tom cleared his throat.

'It was nice of Mr Draper to bring cakes though, wasn't it?'

Sally poked her head out from behind the washing and laughed. 'Nice is one way of looking at it. Bribery is another! But he'll have to think of something other than cake to bribe ME!'

We stared at Sally.

'I'm allergic to gluten!' she explained, cheerfully. 'Haven't eaten a cake since I was fifteen.'

'Not even a nibble?' Tom said, all whispery.

'Not even a crumb. I gave my cake to Anthea.'

Sally disappeared behind a pillowcase. She didn't seem to notice that we had all stopped talking.

'Talking of cakes, do you lot want something to eat? Fig roll? Jammy dodger?'

But for the first time in our lives, we didn't have

time for snacks. We waved goodbye to Sally Merry and raced back through the hedge into Granny's garden, down the side alley and onto Little Draycott. Tom got out his notes.

'So,' he said. 'Out of the eleven members of the parish council, we know that four of them have definitely been poisoned – Granny, Anthony Hodge, Bob Merry and Anthea. Sally Merry hasn't been poisoned, because she didn't eat a cupcake. We also know that Anthea ate two cakes and she has the worst symptoms of all. This is all coming together nicely. We're not allowed to walk to Cudlington on our own so we'll just have to leave those four out of our investigation for now. Which just leaves Mrs Rooney and Louise Fletton in Muddlemoor. Let's go.'

We walked out of Little Draycott and down the main road through the village towards the shop. We were walking past the village hall when Nina and Rupi Mehta overtook us on their bikes. They stopped to say hello.

'You've grown loads,' said Rupi, looking at Tom. 'You have too, Pip.'

She smiled at me and said, 'Hi Joe,' in a NICE voice and I ever so slightly kicked the kerb because I was fed up with being the small one who hadn't grown at all, not even a millimetre.

'We just had an emergency call from Louise Fletton. She's got a sick bug and needs us to babysit her twins.'

I gasped and blurted out, 'It's not a sick bug, she's been poi—' but Tom kicked me before I could say any more.

'What was that?' asked Nina.

'Erm . . .' I said. 'She's been . . . She's been pressured, I mean she's under a lot of pressure!' I said finally and then I pointed at Pip and said, 'Look at Pip's triple backflips!' because Pip was backflipping up the pavement ahead of us.

'Nice,' said Rupi. 'Anyway, we'd better go over to Golders Close. Louise asked us to come as soon as possible.'

They cycled off.

'Sorry,' I said. 'I nearly gave the game away.'

'Don't worry, they didn't notice,' said Tom. 'Plus, they saved us a visit. Now we know that Louise Fletton has been poisoned, we can tick another person off our list.'

We waited outside Mrs Rooney's shop while Tom wrote up his notes. He took ages and I wished I hadn't spent all my pocket money because it would have been nice to buy some sweets to pass the time.

Mrs Rooney was inside the shop, piling up boxes of chocolates behind a sign that said *HALF PRICE*.

'Oh look,' she said. 'It's the sugar fiends.'

She had big bags under her eyes.

'Are you feeling well, Mrs Rooney?' asked Tom, looking up at last.

Mrs Rooney laughed. 'Am I *well*?' she said. 'Am. I. Well? You tell me, young man. I've spent ALL morning unpacking new boxes of food to replace the perfectly GOOD food that is a tiny bit out of date. I've had customers in all morning, wanting to use the post office even though the sign clearly says that the post office doesn't open until two p.m. on Fridays. My back hurts, my feet hurt and I'm behind on the rent. I haven't even stopped for a cup of tea. So, in answer to your question, young man: "Well" is not the word I would use to describe myself at this moment in time, no.'

Tom nodded. 'Sickness? Stomach ache?'

Mrs Rooney stared at Tom for a long time.

'No, my boy,' she said. 'Just a worn-out soul.'

Tom wrote down *Worn-out soul* in his notebook and nodded.

'Very interesting,' he said. 'Mrs Rooney, do you eat cupcakes?'

Mrs Rooney narrowed her eyes.

'And when exactly do you think someone like me has time to eat cake?' she screeched. 'Never, that's when! Now off you hop, before I . . .'

But we ran off before we could hear what she was going to do to us.

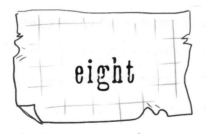

eight

Granny's house smelled of sausages.

'Sally Merry called,' said Granny. 'She said to tell you that Puff came home in the end. Covered in mud, by all accounts. Sally had to give her a bath on her own because poor Bob is feeling very under the weather.'

I gave the others a meaningful nod, a bit like the ones teachers give to each other when they think you aren't looking.

'Goodness!' said Granny. 'You lot look EXTREMELY guilty. What on earth are you up to?!'

But before we could reply, the oven beeped.

'I'm making sausage casserole for later,' said Granny, forgetting she had asked us a question, and then she took one look at our muddy knees and told us to go upstairs for a wash.

Except we didn't have a wash because we were too busy writing up our latest notes.

Proof of the parish council poisoning

Person	Number of poisoned cakes eaten	Symptoms
Granny	1	Mild
Anthea	2	Severe
Mr Hodge	1	Mild
Bob Merry	1	Severe
Sally Merry	0	None
Louise Fletton	Probably 1	Severe
Mrs Rooney	Probably 1	Worn-out soul

'Right, now,' said Tom, 'all the evidence points to a mass poisoning.'

'Children!' called Granny from downstairs. 'You greedy things finished all the milk this morning! But don't worry, I've just remembered that Fergal is giving out free milk tomorrow. Can you remember when he said he'd be open? I'm hoping I can get some in time for breakfast.'

'First thing Saturday morning, I thin—' began Tom. Then he stopped. 'Oh no,' he said to me and Pip. 'The free milk.'

Pip's eyes went really wide.

'It's been staring us in the face all this time,' said Tom, shaking his head.

'What has?' I asked.

Tom flipped back through his notebook.

'Remember what Granny said on the way home from the parish council meeting? About Mr Draper giving away free milk.'

'Yes,' I said, frowning. I still didn't know what Tom meant.

'I think the poisoned cupcakes were just a trial run,'

said Tom. 'I think he's planning to strike again.'

Pip jumped into the splits.

'And this time,' she whispered, 'he's probably going to give them an even bigger dose of poison.'

Straight away I knew Pip was right.

It all made sense. Mr Draper had delayed the vote to give himself more time to poison the parish council properly.

'We need to stop him,' I said.

'But how?' said Tom.

Pip looked up from the splits and went all whispery.

'Easy,' she said. 'We'll just have to break into the farm and steal the poison.'

'But there isn't time. He's giving the milk away tomorrow morning.'

Pip inhaled deeply.

'In that case,' she said. 'We need to steal it *before* tomorrow. We need to break into the farm tonight.'

I looked out of the window and shivered.

'We could set our alarm really early tomorrow

morning instead,' I suggested.

'That won't work,' said Pip. 'Mr Draper is a farmer so he gets up way earlier than most people. Four-thirty a.m. at least.'

'Oh.'

'Pip's right,' said Tom. 'Tonight is our only chance. We'll need our torches. Do you have one, Joe?'

I nodded silently and we found our torches. For the first time in my life I wished my cousins were ever so slightly less brave. The next few hours passed in a blur as I listened to them discussing our plan of action. I tried to distract myself by playing with the Lego on the landing but it was hard to concentrate on Lego with a million thoughts racing in different directions around my head.

'Supper's ready!' called Granny from the bottom of the stairs.

'Coming!' replied Tom. 'And remember,' he whispered to me and Pip as we followed him downstairs. 'Don't say ANYTHING. Act COMPLETELY normal.'

But the problem with being a chatty person is that saying nothing ISN'T normal.

During supper, Granny (who was STILL in her dressing gown) kept glancing at me. 'You're very quiet, Joe,' she said. 'I hope you're not coming down with my sick bug. Early nights for all of us, I think. Me included.'

Tom and Pip pretended to moan about having an early night but they winked at me when Granny was loading the dishwasher. I pushed my sausage casserole away.

A bit later, after watching a few episodes of *Cul-de-Sac*, Granny sent us to bed.

I lay down and closed my eyes because sometimes when you close your eyes, you forget your worries. At least that's what my sister Bella says and she knows what she is talking about because meditation is her new hobby.

'No falling asleep, Joe,' said Tom. 'We need to keep our wits about us. Then, when we're sure Granny is asleep, we can sneak downstairs and escape.'

'What if Mr Draper catches us?' I croaked, trying not to sound as scared as I felt.

Tom cleared his throat.

'It's never a good idea to dwell on your problems,' he said. 'We need to be positive. We need to CONTROL the narrative. The only thing that matters right now is getting the poison away from Mr Draper.'

'OK,' I said. I was pretty certain that controlling the narrative was something you only did in literacy lessons but I didn't say anything just in case I had my facts wrong.

At 9.30 p.m., we heard Granny's footsteps on the stairs. I listened as she brushed her teeth and switched off the stair light. When she opened our door to check on us, none of us moved.

Finally, we heard her cross the landing into her own bedroom. By 10 p.m. her breathing had turned into gentle snores.

Tom leaped out of bed and pulled a hoodie over his pyjamas.

'Come on,' he said. 'It's time.'

Me and Pip grabbed our hoodies and trainers and followed Tom out to the landing. We tiptoed downstairs and unlocked the front door. Then we closed it without making a sound.

In the front garden the air was cold, dark and sweet – like undiluted Ribena. A fleet of clouds floated like huge, dark balloons across the sky, occasionally blocking out the moon.

I ran silently after Tom and Pip. We opened the gate at the end of Granny's path and stepped out on to Little

Draycott. None of us spoke.

The narrow lane seemed longer and wider at night because we couldn't see the edges. It smelled different, too – a combination of wet mud and wild animals – and we even spotted something that might have been a fox. We trudged steadily along the middle of the lane, following the beam of our torches.

I heard a loud crackling sound.

'What was that?' I asked, grabbing hold of Pip.

'Just an old crisp packet,' she whispered, picking it up and putting it in her pocket.

We kept walking until we reached the gate where Pip had filmed Sophie the day before. Behind the gate was Mr Draper's farmyard.

'OK,' hissed Tom. 'Action stations.' He vaulted over the gate and waited for me and Pip to follow him.

The moon sailed out from behind one of the dark clouds and its beam fell across the farmyard, lighting everything up for a few seconds. The yard was surrounded on three sides by old barns and farm buildings. Everything looked broken and shabby, with half-mended roofs and leaking gutters. At the end were three rusty tractors with missing wheels and along one side were stone water troughs full of weeds. Behind the yard was a rickety farmhouse.

In one of the barns I could hear the shuffle of cows.

Tom shone his torch at a wooden shed. The door was bolted. Pip pulled back the bolt and the door swung open, nearly hitting me in the face. I slapped my hand over my mouth to stop myself from shouting out.

Pip and Tom tiptoed through the door and I

followed them. The room was full of junk – broken tractor parts, split buckets, sacks of animal feed, old doors.

'If I was storing poison,' whispered Pip. 'I don't think I'd keep it in here.'

Tom nodded.

'Come on,' he said. 'Let's look for it somewhere else.'

We bolted the door and crossed the farmyard to a newer barn with corrugated metal walls and a metal roof. But just as we reached it, we saw a vehicle approaching the farm from the other side of the gate. We switched off our torches. 'Quick,' Tom hissed. 'Hide!'

We ducked down behind one of the stone water troughs and held our breath. My heart thudded so loudly against my cotton hoodie, I was certain it would be heard over the sound of the engine.

Two headlights approached the gate.

'Look!' I said, forgetting to whisper. 'It's that same white van. The one with the skull and crossbones!'

'*Shhhhhh!*' hissed Tom. 'Someone's coming!'

The door of the farmhouse opened and Mr Draper stomped across the farmyard towards the gate. He spat as he passed our water trough and for a few seconds I could see the flecks of his spit glistening on the stone floor next to my trainer.

'Evening, Harry,' Mr Draper said, reaching the gate. 'Last delivery of the day, is it? Grateful to you, mate.'

The man in the van mumbled something and handed Mr Draper two black bottles.

Mr Draper examined the labels.

'Excellent,' said Mr Draper. 'Didn't order enough yesterday. This job tomorrow is a big one.' He laughed nastily.

'No worries,' said the van man. 'See you next time.'

He climbed back into the driver's seat and reversed back up Little Draycott.

Mr Draper walked back towards us with big, heavy footsteps.

He stopped right next to the water trough we were hiding behind and unlocked the door of the metal

barn. We waited, barely breathing, as he went inside, rummaged around and came out again. He locked the door behind him and walked back to the farmhouse. We waited until his footsteps had become faint and then we peeped out over the water trough. He was no longer carrying the black plastic bottles.

Tom turned to me and Pip.

'Poison,' he said, shaking his head sadly.

'But why does he need MORE?' I asked. 'He had some delivered yesterday.'

'Didn't you hear what he said to the van man? He

didn't order enough for this big job tomorrow.' Tom cleared his throat and pointed at the shed. 'At least we now know where he keeps it. The question is: how do we get inside to steal it?'

We stared at the metal barn. It was grey and shiny and the heavy door was firmly padlocked. Above it was one tiny window.

'Guys,' I whispered, 'maybe we should go back to bed and warn Granny about the milk in the morning.'

Tom stared at the locked door. Pip squinted at the closed window. Neither of them said anything.

'What do you think?' I said. 'It's very late.'

Tom turned to me. His eyes sparkled. The only other time I have seen him look like that was at Christmas when he had a sip of his mum's champagne.

'Too risky,' he said. 'Even if Granny believed us, she would never have time to warn everyone about the milk. We have to stop Mr Draper before someone gets really ill. Before someone *dies*.'

I swallowed silently.

Tom pointed to a gap at the bottom of the metal door. 'We could get in through there.'

The gap was tiny.

'We wouldn't fit!'

'You're right, WE wouldn't. But YOU would, Joe, because you're REALLY small for your age and you haven't grown for ages and you don't have very big muscles.' Tom said this like it was a good thing. 'Joe,' he continued, 'I think you can do it.'

I examined the gap again and swallowed.

'What about the poison though?' I said. 'Even if *I* manage to fit through that tiny gap, how am I going to get the poison out?'

Tom glanced at his watch.

'One thing at a time,' he said, not quite looking me in the eye. 'You just need to be persistent.'

Persistent is probably Tom's favourite word. He got it from his dad, Uncle Marcus, and I know what it means because I looked it up in Mum's dictionary last Christmas. This is what it said:

> **Persistent**
> Continuing in an opinion or course of action in spite of difficulty or opposition.

In other words, it means not giving up, even when things are really tricky.

I took a deep breath and looked at the gap, more carefully this time.

I thought of the poison locked inside the barn. Then I pictured Mr Draper pouring it into containers full of free milk. Finally, I imagined Granny pouring poisoned milk onto her branflakes.

'OK,' I said. 'I'll do it.'

I lay down. The ground beneath my stomach was dusty and cold. It smelled of hay and petrol and something a bit rotten. I stretched my arms out in front of me and placed them under the bottom of the door, through the gap and into the dark beyond.

'Persistence,' I said to myself. 'Persistence.' I closed my eyes and started to wriggle my body underneath the locked door. My arms went under easily but getting my head through was trickier because I had to keep swivelling it from side to side to stop it getting stuck. I felt a bit like a worm trying to cross a busy pavement.

'Ouch!'

I stopped wriggling.

'Are you OK?' asked Tom.

I put my hand up to my face and rubbed something out of the way.

'Crawled into a cobweb.'

'That's good luck, apparently.'

'Oh great.'

I rubbed bits of spider's web out of my eye and twisted my head to the right. I used my legs to push the top half of my body forward, hoping desperately that once my head was through, the rest of me would come easily.

'Ouch!'

'Another cobweb?'

'No, my ear's caught.'

'Blood?'

'Don't think so.'

'Hurry up, then!'

I tilted my head back again, to the left this time, and pushed forward a tiny bit. Then I held my head still and pushed a bit harder.

I felt the concrete floor brush against my stomach as I scrabbled under the locked door. Tiny bits of dust and hay leaped up in the air when I breathed, tickling my eyes. I blinked and looked around. It was dark inside the barn but the moon trickled through the high-up window, turning the flying dust golden.

I kicked my legs like a frog to pull the rest of my body through the gap and stood up. The four walls were lined with neat shelving and on the shelves were bottles and jars and pots and boxes.

'I'm in,' I hissed through the door.

'Well done! Can you see his poison stash?'

I blinked because my eyes were full of dust.

'Haven't looked yet. It's very dark in here. I can't see anything.'

Tom pushed the torch under my door.

'Here,' he said.

'Thanks.'

I picked up the torch and walked around the barn, shining it at the labels on the boxes and bottles piled up on the shelves. There were vitamins for calves and worm medicine for sheep. There were jars and jars of 'linseed oil'. There was a big box of something called 'hoof scrub'.

'Anything?'

I didn't reply because for one thing, I was too busy reading labels and for another thing I didn't want to risk shouting out in case Mr Draper heard me. I tiptoed over to a tall stack of shelves at the back of the shed. It was full of plastic containers with hard-to-read names, such as 'antimicrobials' and 'nonsteroidal anti-inflammatories'. At first I thought these might be scientific words for poison but then I noticed a cartoon picture of a cow smiling in the right-hand corner of the labels and I realised it was more likely to be medicine.

I moved along the shelf and spotted some large black bins. I lifted one of the lids but it was full of grains and seeds, a bit like the stuff that Granny buys to fill the feeders on her bird table. There was no sign of the plastic bottles we'd seen Mr Draper take from the van man and carry into the barn.

'Guys,' I called as quietly as I could. 'I can't find it.'

'*Shhhh!*' hissed Pip and at that moment I heard a dog bark. I froze.

'Rufus has heard us!' said Tom. 'We have to get out of here, Joe. Quick!'

My heart felt squeezed, as if something heavy had fallen off a high diving board right on top of my chest. I tried to take a deep breath but a funny pant came out instead.

'What about the poison?'

No answer.

'Pip?' I called. 'Tom?'

'*Shhhh!*'

I tiptoed towards the door and tried to think of things that made me happy because this sometimes helps me when I am scared to death. I thought of surfing in Devon and the time I got a house point for helping Martha Eliot get her thumb out of the stationery drawer.

'Joe,' said Pip, very quietly. 'Rufus is coming. We're hiding behind the water trough. Find somewhere to hide and we'll let you know when he's gone.'

I went back to the large black feed bins and crouched down behind them.

'Pip?' I whispered. 'Tom?'

They didn't answer.

'Guys?' I whispered again, a bit louder this time.

But the only thing I could hear was more barking and footsteps getting closer.

nine

Once, when I was in Class One, I got locked in the sports shed at lunchbreak. I had only popped in there to try on some of the football boots in Lost Property, just in case they fitted me, but while I was trying them on, Mrs Hollis (who was on playground duty) closed the door and then she locked it because if it isn't locked it keeps opening on its own.

I tried telling Mrs Hollis that I was locked inside but the playground was noisy and Mrs Hollis was wearing a woolly hat over her ears so she couldn't hear very well. No one noticed that I wasn't lining up after break with everybody else but at afternoon register Mr Saunders raised the alarm and then ALL the teachers started a search party. Except, even then, it took them AGES to find me because they kept looking in places where I would never go at break, e.g. the library. Eventually, Louis Steadman told Mr Saunders that he could see a face in the sports shed window and then Mr Saunders ran out into the playground and rescued me.

But even though being locked in the sports shed was quite scary, it was NOTHING compared to being stuck in Mr Draper's barn in the middle of the night.

The sound of heavy boots stopped and the barking got louder.

'What did you hear, eh, Rufus? What is it?'

I heard the sound of a key in the padlock and pulled myself further down behind the black bin. The door creaked open.

'Grrurrrrrr!' barked Rufus, racing straight towards me. I didn't move one muscle, not even my eyelashes.

Mr Draper stomped round the barn. He was so close, that when he coughed I could smell his breath.

'What is it, boy?' he asked Rufus, who was barking at the black bin. 'Smell a rat, can you?'

Mr Draper laughed and I didn't dare breathe.

Bang! A loud clatter came from the farmyard.

'Trespassers!' shouted Mr Draper. 'Outside, Rufus!'

Rufus gave one last growl at my black bin and followed Mr Draper out of the open barn door into the yard.

My legs and arms felt fizzy, as if I had filled them with lemonade. I counted to a hundred, just in case Mr Draper decided to come back. Then I got up very slowly. As I stood up I spotted four black plastic bottles on one of lower shelves. I hadn't noticed them before because they were hidden behind the black bins. They had the words *GRAINGALORE* written across them in green letters.

Underneath *GRAINGALORE* was some smaller red writing that said *WARNING! TOXIC.*

My mouth went dry, a bit like when I eat too many

rice cakes. Until that moment I had not been one hundred per cent certain that Mr Draper was a TRUE-LIFE poisoning murderer. I had slightly hoped that Tom and Pip had got their facts wrong. But now I knew they were right because the one thing I remember from science lessons at school is that toxic is another word for . . .

. . . POISON.

'Tom?' I whispered. 'Pip?'

I heard the faint hoot of an owl but nothing from my cousins.

'I'm just checking the coast is clear!' I said a little more loudly. 'I need your help carrying all this poison!'

Still no reply.

Heavy footsteps came back across the yard towards the barn. I ran back to the black food bin and crouched down.

'Good boy, Rufus,' said Mr Draper. 'You scared those intruders away, good and proper. They were blimmin' fast, though. Didn't get a proper look at them, did we?'

Rufus growled and Mr Draper laughed.

'Next time, maybe, eh! Come on, now. I'll lock up the barn and then we can go to bed.'

The barn door slammed shut, the key turned in the padlock and everything went quiet.

I leaned against the black bin and clenched my fists. I was so cross with myself. I'd had the chance to escape with the poison – and I hadn't taken it.

Now, the only way for me to get out was through the gap under the door. Which would mean leaving the poison behind. And if I did this, Mr Draper would *still* be able to put it in the free milk tomorrow.

I crawled silently to the door of the barn and peeped underneath. The moon seemed higher and brighter than before.

'Tom?' I whispered again. 'Pip?'

Where were they? Had Rufus attacked them? And, if so, were they lying half dead and covered in dog bites?

I almost started wriggling through the gap underneath but I knew I couldn't leave without the

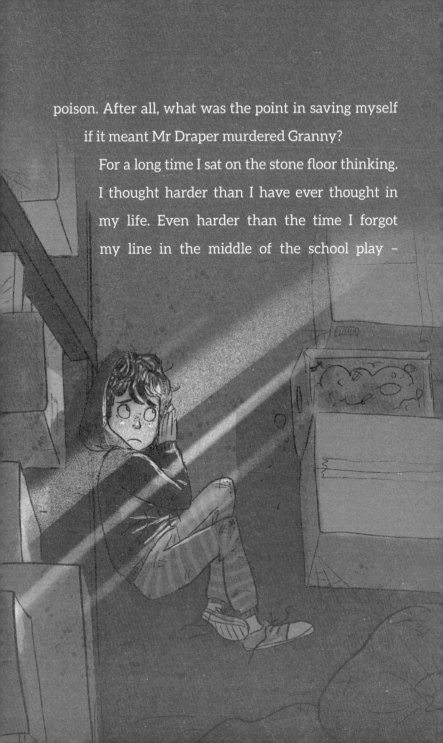

poison. After all, what was the point in saving myself
if it meant Mr Draper murdered Granny?

For a long time I sat on the stone floor thinking.
I thought harder than I have ever thought in
my life. Even harder than the time I forgot
my line in the middle of the school play –

and had to remember before Thea Hastings came on stage.

Finally, after ages, I made up my mind.

I decided that the only thing to do was to stay inside the barn ALL night and then, when Mr Draper came to open the door first thing in the morning, I would dart past him with the poison – just like I dodge past Dylan Moynihan when we play Bulldog at school. Then I would run faster than I have ever run before in my life and I wouldn't stop until I got back to Little Draycott. And – at this point I took a deep breath – if Mr Draper tried to stop me, I would put up a fight. I tried not to worry too much about the fact that there were four bottles of poison to carry and only one of me.

After all that thinking, I felt tired and lay down on the cold floor. Flakes of dust fell from the ceiling into my eyes. A thin trickle of moonlight crept along the concrete floor.

I was cold and lonely and VERY, VERY scared.

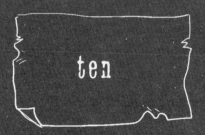

ten

The thing about dreams is that sometimes they can feel completely real.

Like for instance, once I had a dream that Mum had bought me a puppy and the dream was so REAL that in the morning I got up and looked for the puppy in the kitchen and when it wasn't there, I cried.

At some point I must have fallen asleep because I was in the middle of quite a good dream about being a farmer when I heard a *tap, tap, tap*.

I woke up with a jump and leaped to my feet.

For a tiny moment, I hoped it was Granny waking us up for Coco Pops and pancakes but then I remembered that I wasn't tucked up in bed at Granny's house, I was locked in Mr Draper's barn. On my own, with enough poison to murder the whole of Muddlemoor.

It was still dark outside, too dark for it to be morning. My blood tingled like nettle stings. I grabbed the bottles of poison and crouched down to the left of the door. Someone knocked.

Come on, Joe, I told myself firmly. *You can do this.* I stood up on the balls of my feet and got ready to run because that's what Kane Ashfield does at the start of the hundred metres race on Sports Day.

'Are you there?' said an impatient voice, except it didn't sound like Mr Draper, it sounded like someone much younger. It sounded familiar.

'Tom?' I said in a quavery voice.

'Pip thought you might have been murdered by Rufus,' replied Tom cheerfully, 'but I told her it was highly unlikely. We would have heard your screams. Anyway, I'm glad to see that I was correct. Did you like our decoy? We knocked over a wheelbarrow to get Mr Draper out of the barn and away from you.'

My heart felt like it was going to explode.

'I thought you'd been eaten by Rufus,' I said, croaky with relief.

'We were too fast for him,' said Pip. 'But what have you been doing? We've been waiting for you for ages out on the lane.'

'I couldn't leave the poison behind,' I explained and then I told them everything.

'There are four bottles,' I said, 'and if I leave them here, he'll be able to poison the milk. He might even kill Granny! That's why I'm staying till morning. I don't even care if Granny finds out.'

My voice had gone all squeaky, a bit like it does when I am late for football practice and Mum can't find her car keys.

'Wow,' said Pip quietly. 'That's really brave of you, Joe.'

'How do you know for sure it's poison?' asked Tom, and he sounded so bossy and normal, I felt a bit less frightened.

'Because it says *WARNING! TOXIC!* in red letters.'

I expected Tom and Pip to be really shocked or at least slightly impressed but neither of them said anything.

Instead they started scrabbling around outside the door.

'Guys?' I said. 'Are you still there?'

More scrabbling.

'Please don't leave again,' I begged them. 'Please.'

'*Shhh*,' said Tom crossly, 'we don't want Rufus to come sniffing around again. Give me a sec.'

Then came the best sound in the world. Better than everyone cheering when I score a goal. Better than a can of Coke being opened.

It was the sound of a key turning in the padlock.

And then, finally, standing right in front

of me, were Tom and Pip.

'Spare key!' Tom said, grinning. 'Under the doormat. Very poor security of Draper. First place everyone looks.'

My heart stopped feeling like it had been squished. I pushed the poison through the door and then raced over to hug my cousins, trying not to be too noisy and hyper. Tom locked the door and put the key back under the mat, Pip and I picked up the bottles of poison and then we all ran back to Granny's, even faster than Kane Ashfield.

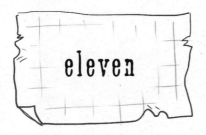

eleven

We slept in until 8:42 a.m. which is an all-time record for me.

'Gosh,' said Granny when we finally came down to breakfast the next morning. 'You've had a long sleep.'

We rubbed our eyes and winked at each other.

'You'll be relieved to know I popped down to Stream Farm while you were sleeping,' said Granny, 'so there's plenty of fresh milk for your cereal.'

I gasped because even though I knew the milk DIDN'T contain poison (because we had stolen it all last night), I STILL didn't feel like pouring it on my Coco Pops – JUST IN CASE. In the end we all just *pretended* to eat our cereal and chucked it in the bin when Granny wasn't looking. Then we raced upstairs with some stolen biscuits to discuss what to do with the poison.

Tom pointed out that we couldn't risk hiding it in our bedroom because sometimes Granny comes in to tidy up and change our sheets.

Pip said we should probably hide it in our usual hiding place, i.e. the weeping willow tree, before Mr Draper found out and started asking questions and me and Tom agreed because we didn't have a better idea.

We got dressed, stuffed the bottles under our jumpers and raced outside.

Once we'd checked that none of the Mehtas were in their garden (which luckily they hardly ever are) we crept inside the weeping willow tree and laid the bottles of poison on the ground next to the trunk. The words *WARNING* and *TOXIC* seemed to glare at us.

Tom got out his notebook and wrote:

Mission Accomplished

Key evidence that proves Fergal Draper is a
poisoning murderer:
Bottles of poison x 4
Poisoned members of the parish council x 5
Film footage of Mr Draper receiving poison x 1

Tom turned to us. 'I'd say we're nearly there.'

I cleared my throat. 'Is it time to spill the beans?'

'No, let's lie low for a bit, keep an eye on Mr Draper
before we do anything drastic.'

'Puff! Puuuuuffffff!'

We peered out of the weeping willow and saw Sally
Merry in her garden, looking for Puff. She was holding
two containers of milk.

'Mr Draper must have been furious when he
discovered the poison was missing,' said Tom. 'Now
he's having to give away perfectly good unpoisoned

milk to all his worst enemies.'

This made me and Pip get the hysterics and we were still laughing when Tom hid the poison under an old picnic rug.

When we got home, Granny told us she was feeling a lot better and asked us if we wanted to help her make a batch of flapjacks.

'I'm ready for anything now!' she said, handing us the mixing bowl. 'Where have you lot been?'

Tom said, 'Chatting,' and I said, 'Playing,' and then we all went bright red and helped ourselves to flapjack mix.

Granny put her head on one side and crinkled her eyes.

'Boredom Cup again?' she asked, winking, and we just smiled because sometimes smiling is easier than telling the whole truth.

When we'd finished baking, Granny said she was planning to order fish and chips for lunch and we cheered because a) we were quite hungry and

b) fish and chips is one of our favourite things to eat, after cereal.

'Good!' said Granny, and she picked up the phone to call the fish and chip shop.

Suddenly everything felt normal and safe. Granny had recovered from being poisoned, Mr Draper's poison supply was safely hidden in the weeping willow, Sophie Pearce was editing the protest films and we were having fish and chips for lunch.

For the first time since Wednesday my heart stopped galloping. I sat down at the kitchen table and watched Tom write up his notes while Pip did pull-ups on the curtain rail. I couldn't help thinking that even though doing investigations is exciting, sometimes it's nice just to mooch around the house not doing much.

'All ordered,' said Granny, putting down the phone. 'And no mushy peas!'

I gave Granny a hug because one thing I love about her is that she always remembers things we don't like to eat, e.g. mushy peas. Granny hugged me back.

'Shoes and coats on then, and we'll get in the car to pick it up.'

The fish and chips tasted delicious and afterwards we wandered around Muddlemoor as if it were the safest village in the UK.

I think Tom was secretly hoping we would bump into Sophie Pearce because he kept saying, 'I wonder what Sophie's doing today,' but we didn't see her protesting at the village hall and she wasn't by the sign in Jeffrey's Meadow or at Mr Draper's gate. I suggested going over to her house on Church Lane to say hello but Tom said, 'We can't do that!' in the same shocked voice that grown-ups use when you suggest having sweets for breakfast.

Later on in the afternoon, Anthea and Mr Hodge popped round for tea because they had finally recovered from their poisoning. We had to sit at the kitchen table with them and Mr Hodge spent half an hour telling everyone about the different shapes of Roman spears.

'Honestly, Anthony,' said Anthea, 'thanks to you, none of us will ever need to go to the British Museum again!'

'Oh, but you must go, Anthea, it's a completely different experience seeing artefacts in the flesh.'

Anthea laughed. 'I can't imagine it could be half as *fascinating* though,' she said and winked at us over the top of her tea cup.

'Has everybody else in the council recovered from the sick bug?' asked Granny.

'Seems so,' replied Anthea, 'although I haven't seen Bob Merry yet. Either way, there should definitely be enough of us to vote against Fergal's fiasco on Monday.'

Granny sighed. 'I don't know,' she said, 'perhaps we should just let him get on with it. After all, it *is* his land.'

'Jenny!' shrieked Anthea. 'Where's your backbone?'

And Granny said, 'Back in the nineteen seventies, most probably,' and then they all got the hysterics and

started talking about the olden days.

But we aren't very interested in the nineteen seventies, so we escaped into the garden to play football.

'Hello, children,' said Sally Merry, peering over the hedge. 'Puff's run off again. I don't suppose you've seen her, have you?'

We shook our heads.

'Oh dear,' said Sally, 'I hope she hasn't gone back to Fergal's. I'm worried he might do something nasty to Puff if she keeps bothering Rufus.'

I was about to tell Sally that not even a horrible man like Mr Draper would want to harm an innocent dog like Puff but then Tom told us about a dog called Rex who chased a sheep and was shot by an angry farmer.

I didn't say anything for a few seconds because this was one of the most shocking things I had ever heard and I could tell that Sally Merry thought so too because she chewed her lip and said, 'I don't THINK Puff would chase livestock, but then she has been rather peculiar lately.'

'Do you want us to go and look for her?' I asked, to change the subject, and Sally said, 'Oh, would you? Bob's a lot better today but I hate leaving him on his own when he's feeling poorly. Thank you, children, you ARE kind.'

We looked everywhere for Puff. We went to the church and the playground. We walked up to the allotments and searched behind all the sheds. We went into Golders Close. We even walked (well, sprinted) down The Gravels, the haunted shortcut in the middle of Muddlemoor that we NEVER go down if we can help it. We came out at the village shop. We still didn't have any money but I volunteered to go in, just in case Mrs Rooney was in a good mood and wanted to give us a Mr Freeze for free.

Mrs Rooney was at the counter, watching TV. 'I hope you haven't come here to complain,' she said. 'I've had half the village moaning at me recently. For the record, I only sell the best quality produce and that is a fact. Understood?'

I nodded and Mrs Rooney slapped a reduced-price box of chocolates down on the counter.

'You after these?' she said.

'Erm,' I said, because we didn't have enough money for chocolates, even though they were half price. 'We were actually wondering if you had any spare Mr Freezes that you might be giving away for free.'

Mrs Rooney sniffed loudly and I tried smiling kindly because Mum always tells me that smiling is a safe thing to do when someone is cross.

'Are you laughing at me?' she said crossly, advancing.

'No,' I said, backing out of the shop.

'Some people!' said Mrs Rooney. 'As if the complaining wasn't bad enough, I've now got Fergal Draper giving away free milk – which means no one bought any milk from me this morning. The cheek!'

She sighed and slammed the door.

I joined Tom and Pip on the bench opposite the shop.

'She's in a very bad mood,' I told them. 'Says she's fed up with people complaining and fed up with

Mr Draper giving away free milk. She thought I was laughing at her.'

Pip looked thoughtful.

'What about the Mr Freezes?' asked Tom.

'No chance.'

We sighed and wandered back to the Merrys', to see if Puff had turned up. And that's when I heard something coming from Ronnie Mehta's garden.

'Did you hear that?'

'What?' said Tom.

'I think it's Puff!' I said, leaping through the hedge.

Loud rustling was coming from the weeping willow tree. I ran over and dived through the branches.

Puff was in the middle of our hiding place, right next to the tree trunk. As soon as she saw me she jumped up and knocked me over. Then she wagged her tail.

'Found her!' I called out to the others, and a few seconds later Tom and Pip crashed through the branches. When they saw Puff they started laughing with relief and for a few seconds none of us could stop laughing, partly because we were really pleased to see Puff but mainly because it meant we didn't have to go and look for her at Mr Draper's farm.

But then I noticed that Puff was chewing on something and when I saw what it was I stopped laughing and started to panic.

Because the thing in Puff's mouth was a plastic bottle with the words WARNING and TOXIC printed in red writing.

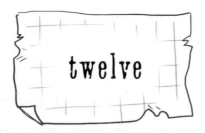

twelve

I have no idea how Pip managed to get that bottle of poison out of Puff's mouth but she did.

Puff ran off and Pip placed the bottle carefully on the ground in front of us.

Straight away I noticed that the bottle was covered in tiny dents and toothmarks from where Puff had chewed it.

'What if some of the poison seeped out and got in Puff's mouth?' I asked. And we all closed our eyes because this was the worst thing that had ever happened to us, by a HUNDRED MILES.

'Are we ... are we dog murderers?' asked Pip.

'Well,' said Tom in his serious voice, 'we can't rule it out.'

'If Puff dies,' I said, 'I will NEVER forgive myself for the rest of my life.'

And I meant it.

I wanted to go and warn Bob and Sally Merry straight away but Tom got out his notebook and turned to the page where he had written down the symptoms.

Signs and symptoms of poisoning

The symptoms of poisoning will depend on the type of poison and the amount taken in, but general things to look out for include:

drowsiness

vomiting

stomach pains

confusion

'Puff wasn't showing any symptoms,' he said. 'Maybe none of the poison leaked out. Let's keep an eye on her. If she starts showing more than one symptom, then we'll tell Bob and Sally.'

'But what about the poison?' I asked, because I didn't fancy leaving it under the weeping willow tree in case Puff or another animal decided to chew on it.

'Yes, the poison incriminates us,' said Tom. 'Let's put it in Granny's wheelie bin. The bin men come on Mondays, so all evidence against us should be gone before anyone finds out.'

I gasped. 'That's *destroying* evidence. It's what true-life murderers do.'

'I know,' said Tom. 'But we didn't mean to poison Puff. We were trying to save Muddlemoor. And now we need to save ourselves.'

We put the bottles of poison carefully under our jumpers and carried them through the gardens, back to Granny's. The lid of the wheelie bin was quite high up and hard to open. Plus we had to keep hiding behind it every time somebody walked past. But eventually we managed to get the bottles of poison into the bin and close the lid.

By now we were really tired and all we wanted

to do was to go back to Granny's to watch TV but we knew we had to go back to the Merrys' to find out if Puff was showing any symptoms of poisoning. But just as we were climbing through the hedge into the Merrys' garden, we heard shouting coming from Jeffrey's Meadow.

Mr Draper was sitting in a huge digger and he was digging a large ditch along the edge of the field. On the ground in front of the digger, was Sophie Pearce shouting, 'Shame on you!' in a really loud voice. We ran towards her.

'Sophie!' I shouted over the noise of the digger. 'What's happening?'

Sophie looked FURIOUS.

'He's breaking the rules, that's what's happening,' she said. 'He's digging the foundations for his chicken farm which he's not allowed to do until the parish council votes in favour.'

The noise of the digger got louder.

'Out of my way, kids,' shouted Mr Draper from his

high-up seat. 'This is a big digger and I don't want to accidentally run over one of you.'

Sophie Pearce shook her fist.

'You're not going to get away with this,' she said. 'The people of Muddlemoor will NEVER let you build a chicken farm here.'

Mr Draper laughed and put his foot on the digger's accelerator.

'We'll see about that, princess! They seemed to like their free milk this morning.'

Sophie Pearce shook her head.

'I'm not a princess,' she said, furiously. Then she turned to us and said, 'I need to be where HE isn't. See you guys at the meeting on Monday.'

After Sophie had gone, Mr Draper started digging another wide ditch just alongside us. The tyres came so close that our faces and clothes got splattered with mud.

'Hey!' said Tom. 'Watch it!'

'YOU watch it,' said Mr Draper. 'You're on my land.

Go on, go home to Grandma before I accidentally run over you!'

Even though we were pretty sure that Mr Draper was joking, we decided not to risk finding out if he definitely was. The problem was, to get back to Granny's we now had to jump over the ditch that Mr Draper had just dug. And the tricky thing about jumping ditches is that it's easier than it looks, especially if your legs are on the short side.

Pip and Tom jumped over easily but I fell and landed with a thud at the bottom. The ditch smelled of worms and rusty gates and rainwater. When I stood up I couldn't see over the top. Huge clods of mud stuck to the bottom of my trainers.

'Are you hurt?' asked Pip.

'I'm stuck!' I said. I tried to climb out but the sides were too steep and I slid straight back down again.

Tom stretched out his arm.

'Can you reach me?'

I stood on my toes and felt the tips of my fingers

brush against Tom's hand.

'Just. I'll jump up if you get ready to grab on to me.'
But just as I was about to jump I spotted something
glinting in the mud next to my feet.

'Hang on a sec,' I said, and crouched down. Sticking
out of the mud were six large coins. They were about
the size of two pound coins but I couldn't be a hundred
per cent sure what they were because even when I
pulled them out of the ground and wiped the mud
off, they were covered in a thick layer of rusty green.
But I didn't care about the mud because all I could think
was that, finally, we had some money of our own to
buy sweets and Mr Freezes at Mrs Rooney's.

'Joe!' said Tom. 'What are you doing?'

I started explaining about the money but Tom
and Pip couldn't hear me over the sound of
the digger.

'Never mind,' I said, pocketing the coins.
'Just pull me out,' and I jumped. Tom
and Pip grabbed my hands and pulled.

I put my foot against the side of the ditch and pushed. Then, finally, after quite a bit of scrambling, I made it to the top.

I was so relieved to be on our way home, I forgot all about the money in my pocket.

As soon as Granny saw us, she ran us a bath, put our clothes in the washing machine and made us our tea and hot chocolates. 'How on earth did you manage to get so muddy?' she asked, so I told her about Mr Draper digging up Jeffrey's Meadow.

'But he's not allowed to do that before the vote,' she said and went to phone Anthea.

While Granny was on the phone, we decided to sneak out to check on Puff, even though we normally watch telly after tea.

We slipped through the hedge into the Merrys' garden and when we got to their kitchen window, we stood on tiptoes and peeped through.

Puff was in her basket in a corner of the Merrys' kitchen.

'Phew!' I said when I spotted her but then I looked more closely and said, 'Oh,' because Puff wasn't wriggling or panting or wagging her tail or doing any of the things she usually does. She was lying in her basket with her legs in the air. And she wasn't moving.

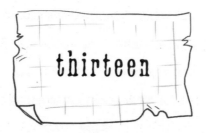

thirteen

One thing I've never done either on purpose OR accidentally is harm a living creature.

Like for instance, once, when we were on holiday in Greece, a mosquito got caught in my bedroom but I wouldn't let Mum squish it even though it was trying to bite me. I had to stay up ALL night because it was the only way I could make sure the mosquito didn't bite me, except I must have fallen asleep eventually because when I woke up in the morning the mosquito wasn't there and I was COVERED in red bites. But I was STILL glad that Mum hadn't squished it because in my opinion ALL living creatures are better alive than dead – even ones that bite.

When I saw Puff with her legs in the air I just

KNEW that she must have drunk some of the poison and after that I couldn't sleep a wink ALL NIGHT because I was so worried.

On Sunday morning, instead of waiting for Tom and Pip to wake up, I tried sneaking out of the house at 6.03 a.m. to check on Puff. But Granny heard me opening the kitchen door and said, 'Hold it right there, buster!' just like a detective in a film, and then she made me eat a bowl of cereal because at Granny's we aren't allowed out until we've eaten a proper breakfast.

While I was eating, Tom and Pip came down, so I had to wait for them to eat their breakfast too but even after they had finished, I couldn't go and check on Puff because Granny asked us to do some jobs, e.g. hanging up washing on the line in the garden and tidying up the Lego. Then, when we'd finished all our jobs, Granny offered to take us to the adventure playground.

I said, 'Do we have to?' (because right now checking on Puff mattered even more than wooden drawbridges) but Granny said, 'Joe Robinson, I hope you're JOKING!'

and I had to pretend that I was because I'd been asking Granny about going to the adventure playground all week and I didn't want to hurt her feelings.

On our way to the car we bumped into Bob and Sally Merry, who were walking to church. The first thing I noticed was that they didn't have Puff with them and my stomach went all funny because Sally and Bob always take Puff EVERYWHERE, including church.

'Oh, hello you lot,' said Sally. 'Thanks for looking for Puff yesterday. You'll be glad to know that she came back on her own in the end. But she must have had one heck of an adventure because she's been asleep ever since.'

I gripped Pip's hand because drowsiness was one of the symptoms of poisoning.

Tom glared at us and cleared his throat. 'Is she OK otherwise?' he asked. 'No vomiting, no stomach pains?'

Sally laughed.

'I think you're muddling Puff up with Bob!'

Bob nodded weakly and I think he must have noticed our worried faces because he said, 'I'm much better now, thanks, children.'

'Would you say Puff is FINE?' I asked.

Bob and Sally smiled because Puff is their favourite topic of conversation. They like talking about her even more than they like talking about their holiday house in Italy.

'Well, now that you mention it, she isn't a hundred per cent, is she, Sal?'

'Nooo,' said Sally, thoughtfully. 'She's rather off her food.' She paused. 'But to be honest with you, this is probably a good thing. I'm afraid we've let Puff get RATHER LARGE recently!'

Bob smiled and said, 'Well, we do spoil her!' and Sally said, 'Just a bit!' and then they both laughed and hurried off because they didn't want to be late for church.

As we climbed into Granny's car, none of us said one word. We just gulped.

The adventure playground is normally one of our favourite places but that morning we were too worried about Puff to have fun. After half an hour, I asked Granny if we could go home.

'Good heavens!' said Granny, looking surprised. 'I thought we'd be here all morning.' And we just shrugged our shoulders because we didn't want to give the game away.

As soon as we got back we raced into the garden because we wanted to climb through the hedge to check on Puff, but Granny followed us outside to get the washing in.

'Oh dear!' she said when she spotted the large rectangle of ditches in the middle of Jeffrey's Meadow. 'He's completely butchered that lovely field.'

I told Granny not to give up hope (because that is what Mum always tells me when e.g. I don't think I'm going to get picked for the Year Four badminton tournament) but Granny just patted me on the back and said, 'You can't win them all, Joe,' in a sad voice and went inside to make Sunday lunch.

The Merrys were still at church so we hopped through the hedge and walked up to the back of their house.

Puff was curled up in her basket but when I called her name through the patio doors, she rolled over slowly and blinked. I breathed a sigh of relief because at least she was still alive but then Pip pointed out that Puff might just be dying really slowly because that is what happens to mice when Uncle Marcus poisons them. I asked Pip if she was sure about this and she said, 'When mice are poisoned it takes them a few days to die because their insides explode in slow motion.' And at that point I felt really dizzy and had to go back to Granny's for something to drink.

For the rest of the morning, I kept picturing horrible things in my head, e.g. poisoned dogs with exploding insides, and I was so worried about Puff that I could only eat a tiny bit of roast chicken at lunch.

'Off your food again?' said Granny, feeling my head as I flopped down on the sofa and all I could do was nod.

Granny said in that case I had to stay in and rest, so after lunch Tom and Pip went back to check on Puff without me. Pip took some leftover roast chicken so they could test if Puff had lost her appetite (loss of appetite is another symptom of poisoning) and Tom took his notebook because he had started writing up a new section called *Puff and the Poison*.

It seemed like they were gone for AGES and I was starting to get pretty bored, when they burst through the sitting room door and sat down next to me.

'Pip pushed tiny bits of roast chicken through the letter box,' said Tom, 'and Puff didn't even NIBBLE it.'

'Did she sniff it?' I asked, because I know for a fact that NO dog can resist the smell of roast chicken.

'Yes, but then she walked back to her basket and went to sleep.'

I lay back on the sofa and asked Tom if I could have a look at his notebook. I turned to the page where he had written the symptoms of poisoning:

drowsiness
vomiting
stomach pains
confusion

I read the page three times and said, 'Even if we're not telling the police, we need to tell Bob and Sally.'

Tom and Pip nodded.

'Are you feeling well enough?' said Tom, and I said, 'As well as I'll ever feel in the circumstances,' and then we sneaked out of the house before Granny could stop us. But even before we got to the end of Granny's front path, Pip said, 'OH NO!' in an emergency voice and pointed to a van parked outside the Merrys' house.

The van was bright red and it had high-vis yellow stripes across the roof. Written on the side in bright blue letters were the words *EMERGENCY VET.*

We crept up to the Merrys' front path and listened at the door. Inside the house, Sally was crying and saying, 'Oh Puff!' over and over again.

And that's when I knew our luck had run out.

fourteen

The walk from the Merrys' front door back to Granny's normally takes us about eighteen seconds but that Sunday it seemed to last for ever. We didn't feel like rushing. We didn't feel like doing anything. We were ninety-nine point nine per cent certain that Puff had died and we were a hundred per cent certain it was all our fault.

None of us spoke.

All I wanted was to be back in my tiny bedroom in London as far away from Muddlemoor as possible.

'Hello, Terrible Trio!'

Anthea was walking up Little Draycott towards Granny's. She was holding a box of chocolates out in front of her and at first I thought she was going to offer one to us but when I moved closer to have a look, she whisked them away.

'Is your grandmother in?' she said, flinging open the gate without waiting for an answer.

We trudged slowly alongside her.

'Goodness!' she said, spotting our worried faces. 'Has someone died?'

I put my hands over my mouth and Pip and Tom's noses went all flarey.

'Fishy business!' said Anthea and waltzed inside Granny's house, shouting 'Yoohoo!' at the top of her voice.

'Gosh, more chocolates!' said Granny, coming into the hall. 'Anthony gave me some of those last week.'

'Did he now?' Anthea gritted her teeth. 'Bought half price from Mrs Rooney, no doubt?'

Granny stretched out her hand to take the box. 'Thank you, Anthea, how kind of you!'

'Careful!' said Anthea. 'Eat them at your peril.'

Granny took off her washing-up gloves.

'Good heavens! What on earth do you mean?'

Anthea cleared her throat and glanced at us.

'I think we should probably get ourselves out of earshot, if you catch my drift.'

'Ah,' said Granny, nodding. 'Good idea.'

She led Anthea into the kitchen and shut the door. We didn't move. Pip put her ear against the kitchen door and listened.

'They're whispering,' she said. 'But I can't hear any actual words.'

A chair scraped across the floor.

'Out you go, children!' called Granny from inside the kitchen. 'It's far too nice an afternoon for you to be shut up indoors.'

We didn't move.

'Go on!' said Granny again. 'I need to have a private

chat with Anthea for a few minutes.'

We trudged through the hall, opened the front door and went to sit on the garden wall. The emergency vet ambulance was still outside the Merrys' house.

'Should we confess now?' I asked.

'Probably,' said Tom, nodding.

But none of us moved.

Pip said, 'The moment we TELL them that we've poisoned Puff then everybody in Muddlemoor will hate us and we won't be welcome here ever again and I'll have to go to art club in the holidays instead.'

She wiped her nose on her sleeve and for a few minutes we all just sat there silently because the thought of this being our last EVER visit to Muddlemoor was a TRAGEDY.

After a while, Granny's front door opened and Anthea stepped out onto the doorstep. 'Cheerio, Jenny,' she said. Then she said, 'OK if I chuck the chocolates of doom in your wheelie bin?'

'Feel free,' said Granny, shutting the front door.

Anthea set off down the front path. She opened the lid of Granny's wheelie bin, threw away the box of chocolates and started to walk away.

But before we could go and rescue the box of chocolates (because when it comes to chocolates we are not keen on waste), Anthea stopped and frowned.

She walked back towards the bin, opened the lid and ...

... pulled out a black bottle of poison.

Sometimes there is only one thing to do and that is run for your life.

Together we leaped off the wall, ran through the front door and raced upstairs to our bedroom.

We flung ourselves on top of our beds and waited.

'Jenny!' called Anthea from the front garden. 'Come out here at once!'

We crept out of our bedroom and peered through the landing banister.

Granny rushed out of the kitchen and into the front garden.

'Anthea?' she said, walking over to the wheelie bin. 'What is it?'

Anthea held up the bottles of poison. She showed them to Granny. 'This!' she said. '*This* is what's going on!'

Granny put on her glasses and examined the label.

'Now, you *know* how I feel about chemical fertilisers,' said Anthea crossly. 'I can't allow you to enter Muddlemoor's Best Grown contests this summer

if you've been treating your flowers and vegetables with this stuff. Muddlemoor is an ORGANIC village, remember, Jenny. Using chemicals is CHEATING.'

'I know that, Anthea,' said Granny, peering at the bottle. 'I wouldn't dream of using chemical fertiliser in my garden. These bottles aren't mine.'

Anthea frowned.

'Then what were they doing at the bottom of

your wheelie bin?'

'I haven't the foggiest.'

At that point, we started tiptoeing back towards our bedroom but Anthea said, 'Hold it RIGHT there, you lot!' and then she shouted, 'OUTSIDE PRONTO!' Reluctantly, we stomped downstairs, crossed the hall and joined Granny and Anthea in the front garden.

'Do you lot have some explaining to do?' asked Granny, and even though Tom kept kicking me in the ankle, I said, 'Um,' because a) I am not a very good fibber and b) I was a bit tired of having to keep secrets.

Granny put her hands on her hips and told us to explain EVERYTHING 'from the top' (which means the beginning) but the problem was, none of us wanted to admit stealing poison and we definitely didn't want to admit that we had accidentally MURDERED Puff. Because Pip was right: if anyone found out about what we'd done, we would NEVER be welcome in Muddlemoor again.

We stood next to the wheelie bin, staring at our

toes and nibbling our fingernails. And none of us said ONE WORD about ANYTHING – not even when Granny tried to bribe us with Jaffa Cakes.

Eventually Granny told us to go inside and tidy our room, even though it was still the afternoon, and I could tell she was REALLY disappointed with us because she kept shaking her head and saying, 'Honestly!'

But even though we hated making Granny cross, we were still glad we hadn't spilled the beans because it only would have made her crosser.

We sat on our beds, feeling miserable.

'Our whole investigation started because we wanted to SAVE animals' lives,' I said, 'and now we've ended up doing the opposite of saving, i.e. killing.'

And then I stopped talking because for the first time in my life I had run out of anything to say.

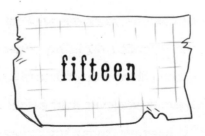

fifteen

Our bedroom clock seemed to turn in slow motion. We sat on our beds for what seemed like hours and none of us said a word because we were so busy worrying.

Eventually, after ages, there was a knock on the door.

'Hello, you lot!' said Granny. 'You appear to have gone to ground.'

Anthea switched on our bedroom light and stared at us, all frowny.

'No, we were just . . . erm . . . we were thinking,' I began, but I stopped when I saw what they were holding: Tom's notebook and Pip's video camera.

For a few seconds the WHOLE room was DEADLY quiet. Granny cleared her throat.

'We simply couldn't work out why four bottles of chemical fertiliser ended up in my wheelie bin,' she said, 'so we've been doing a bit of detective work of our own.' She paused. 'And clever Anthea has managed to join all the dots together. Once a spy, always a spy.'

Anthea grinned and flicked through Tom's notebook.

'Excellent clue-keeping, children,' she said. 'And, dogged investigating, too. But you were so busy focusing on Fergal Draper, you missed one small clue that was there right from the start.'

We gulped.

'Does this look like a normal box of chocolates to you?' Anthea asked, holding up the chocolates she'd thrown away in the wheelie bin.

'Er, yes,' said Tom.

'No!' said Anthea. 'This is NOT a normal box of chocolates. This is a VERY OLD box of chocolates. This is, in fact, a box of chocolates that is THREE YEARS past its sell-by date.'

I glanced at Tom and Pip and was relieved that they

looked just as puzzled as I felt.

Anthea sighed. 'Oh, do keep up, I had you lot down as half-decent investigators!' She cleared her throat. 'Mrs Rooney has been selling these gone-off chocolates at half price since Wednesday. They've been flying off her shelves of course, because not only do the good people of Muddlemoor have a thing for salted caramels – they have even more of a thing for a bargain!' She paused. 'Are you with me?'

'Erm,' I said, and chewed my lip.

'These chocolates are way past their sell-by date,' explained Anthea in a slow and careful voice, 'which is why everyone got sick when I unwittingly took a box of gone-off chocolates to last week's parish council meeting (well, everybody except Sally Merry, who didn't eat any). Your poisoner isn't Fergal Draper, it's Mrs Rooney. She's accidentally food poisoned half the village!'

Until now, me, Tom and Pip had been looking at the floor but the moment Anthea said the word 'poisoned', we looked up and stared at her with our mouths wide open.

'Ha! NOW I've piqued their interest!' said Anthea, roaring with laughter.

Granny examined the box of chocolates.

'The funny thing is,' she said, 'they tasted fine. Delicious, in fact. Which is why NONE of us realised they had gone off. Thank goodness everybody has recovered from the food poisoning.'

'They haven't fully,' said Anthea. 'Some people

are still below par – Bob Merry is off his food, the Cudlington contingent are still pretty bad, I hear, and Louise Fletton has been in bed for days. The Mehta girls are babysitting her twins twenty-four-seven.'

Granny shook her head. 'Well, thank goodness nobody died, anyway.'

'Indeed,' agreed Anthea. 'That would have been Death by Chocolate of the very worst kind.'

Granny burst out laughing and Anthea joined in and then they both got hysterics and had to lean against the walls to recover.

'Oh dear,' said Granny, wiping her eyes. 'It really isn't funny. How is Mrs Rooney dealing with the news?'

'She's under investigation. Health and Safety have been on the phone, lecturing her about food hygiene. She's worried they might take away her shopkeeper's licence.'

'Oh dear!' said Granny. 'Muddlemoor wouldn't be the same without Mrs Rooney.'

'Well, it hasn't come to that yet,' said Anthea. 'But

between you and me, that shop will be under strict supervision for months, if not years.'

'Poor Mrs Rooney,' said Granny, and then she muttered, 'Death by Chocolate!' and started giggling all over again.

Me, Tom and Pip didn't laugh. We didn't even smile. For one thing, being food poisoned is not exactly a laughing matter and for another thing, if Mrs Rooney was the REAL Muddlemoor poisoner then we had committed a true-life burglary and ACCIDENTALLY poisoned Puff for NO REASON.

I think I may have slightly fainted because the next minute, Granny was sitting on the corner of my bed with her hand on my forehead.

'You look VERY pale, Joe,' she said. 'I expect you are worried about Puff?'

I gasped because I couldn't bear Granny to find out about what we had done to Puff. 'We didn't mean to murder her!' I said in a really squeaky voice and then I burst into tears.

Granny put her arm round me and gave me a long hug. She smelled of gardens and perfume. I leaned against her cardigan and wished I could go to sleep and never think about Puff for the rest of my life.

'But you didn't murder Puff,' she said in a kind voice.

I stopped crying. 'What?' I sniffed.

Granny smiled.

'Anthea and I have just been on the phone to Sally Merry. You were right about SOME things. Puff HAS been rather drowsy lately and she DID lose her appetite, but none of this is because she was poisoned. It was because she was PREGNANT!'

Even though I am known for being a chatterbox, I sometimes forget how to speak. I swallowed and stared and closed my eyes to check I wasn't dreaming.

Granny laughed.

'I thought you'd be pleased,' she said. 'Not even Sally or Bob knew about Puff. At least they didn't until this afternoon when Puff gave birth to FIVE PERFECT PUPPIES.'

An invisible weight seemed to lift from my chest and stomach and float out of the window. 'Are you sure?' I asked.

'A hundred per cent,' said Granny and then she ruffled my hair and gave me another hug. 'The vet's just left in his emergency van.'

'They're pretty certain that Rufus is the father,' said Anthea, laughing, 'although I somehow doubt that Fergal Draper will be helping to pay the vet's bill.'

Straight away I remembered about Puff running off with Rufus and how Sally Merry had said it had been going on for months. Suddenly everything made sense.

'Are you sure Puff didn't eat any poison?'

'Positive,' said Anthea. 'These bottles of Graingalore are made from reinforced plastic. Terrible for the environment of course, but you'd need bigger canines than Puff's to puncture a hole in one of these bad boys.'

I let out a long sigh.

'You'll have to take these bottles back to Mr Draper and apologise for stealing them,' said Granny. 'It's chemical fertiliser, not poison. He will have bought it to make his corn grow, to feed all those poor battery chickens he's about to invest in.'

'But it says TOXIC on the bottles,' Pip whispered. 'Toxic means poisonous.'

'Well,' said Granny, 'the chemicals he uses *are* pretty poisonous. You wouldn't want to eat the stuff, that's for sure. But lots of farmers use it on their crops.'

'What about the van it was delivered in?' asked Tom. 'It had a skull and crossbones on the side.'

Anthea chuckled. 'Ah yes, the video footage.' She paused and looked at us. 'Pip's camerawork was first-rate but I'm afraid what you thought was a skull and crossbones is actually a logo for Round the World – the very well-known delivery company.' She got out her

phone and tapped a few buttons. 'Look, that's the earth, not a skull,' she said, holding up her phone so we could see her screen. 'And what you thought were crossed bones is actually a compass, showing all the different directions Round the World takes.'

For a few minutes our bedroom was really quiet while we let everything sink in. Mr Draper hadn't tried to poison the parish council. We hadn't killed Puff. Best of all, Puff had given birth to five puppies.

I looked at Tom and Pip and smiled. Not even the thought of having to visit Mr Draper and explain about stealing his fertiliser could ruin our mood.

'What do the puppies look like?' I asked, because when it comes to puppies, I could talk for hours.

But Granny told us she had to start making tea and Anthea said she was going home to start preparing for the parish council meeting tomorrow morning and at that point, our good mood WAS ruined because even though we were ECSTATIC about Puff's puppies, we still hadn't managed to save the battery chickens.

And, after all, saving chickens was the reason we had started the whole investigation in the first place.

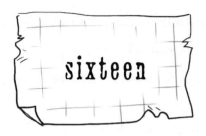

sixteen

Monday morning was warm and sunny.

As soon as we'd cleared up breakfast, we wanted to go and see Puff's puppies but Granny said Bob and Sally weren't ready for visitors yet and then she told us we had to give them some space.

Grown-ups are very keen about having space around them and some teenagers are too. In my opinion having space around you is not one bit interesting but I didn't bother saying any of this to Granny because once, when I tried explaining the exact same thing to Bella, she locked me out of her bedroom.

'Who will keep an eye on Puff and her puppies when Bob and Sally go and vote at the meeting this

morning?' I asked (because I was secretly hoping they might ask us) but Granny said, 'Oh Bob and Sally aren't coming to the meeting. They don't want to leave the puppies.'

'But what about the chicken farm?' said Tom. 'Every vote counts!' And I could tell he was thinking of Sophie Pearce more than chickens because he started flicking his hair.

'Yes, it's terrible timing,' said Granny. 'But it can't be helped. Right now, newborn puppies are more important than chicken farms – at least, they are to Bob and Sally.'

Tom asked Granny if all the other members of the parish council had recovered from food poisoning enough to vote, e.g. Louise Fletton and the people who lived in Cudlington.

'I'm not sure,' said Granny. 'We'll find out when we get there. But with the Merrys not coming, I think the vote is going to be very close.'

I looked out of the window at Jeffrey's Meadow, all

dug-up and muddy from Mr Draper's digger. It was sad to think that the next time we visited Granny, there might not be a meadow there at all, just a big barn full of caged chickens.

'If Mr Draper wins the vote, will he be able to build his farm straight away?' I asked.

Granny nodded. 'I'm afraid so. Which is why we MUSTN'T be late for this meeting. We're leaving in five minutes, so you'd better get dressed and brush your teeth in record time.'

We set off up the stairs. 'And make sure you wear clean clothes!' Granny called after us. 'There's a laundry basket of washing on the landing.'

I rummaged around in the laundry basket to find my favourite jeans and hoodie but I may have slightly forgotten to brush my teeth because when I raced back down, Granny said, 'That really WAS record time!' and sent me back upstairs.

And then Pip couldn't find her trainers and Tom had to go to the toilet and by the time we left Granny's house it was almost 9 a.m. I wanted to peep through the Merrys' window to see if we could glimpse Puff and her puppies but Granny said we had to run all the way to the village hall because we were late.

When we burst through the doors, the meeting had already started.

'I'm so sorry!' said Granny.

'No excuses!' said Anthea, and then she said, 'Step on it, Jenny,' and twiddled her thumbs impatiently.

Anthea was sitting at a large rectangular table on top

of a raised platform at the end of the room. Also at the table were Mr Hodge, Mrs Rooney and Louise Fletton, along with a few people we didn't know.

'Members of the parish council are up here – that's you, Jenny. Terrible Trio, find yourselves a chair in the front row where we can keep an eye on you.'

The village hall looked a bit like my school sports hall, except there wasn't any lost property piled in the corner and it didn't smell of lunch.

'Over here!' whispered Sophie Pearce. She was

sitting on the front row next to her parents. Further along the row were Mr and Mrs Draper and Rufus.

Mr Draper scowled at us when we sat down and I suddenly got butterflies in my stomach because I remembered about having to return his bottles of poison and apologise.

All around us people were talking about the food poisoning and I heard Mrs Rooney say, 'I know my name's mud round here,' but when Anthea stood up, everybody stopped talking and listened.

'This meeting is about the proposed intensive chicken farm on Jeffrey's Meadow, Muddlemoor,' Anthea said. 'If Muddlemoor parish council votes in favour of the chicken farm, then the applicant, Mr Fergal Draper of Stream Farm, will be able to start building the farm with immediate effect. If the parish council votes against the farm, then Mr Draper will have to make an appeal to Stonely Council. Understood?'

Everybody nodded, except Sophie Pearce, who kept

looking nervously at the door.

'Good,' said Anthea. 'In that case, before the parish council vote, Mr Draper would like to say a few words about his plans.' Anthea sat down with her clipboard.

Mr Draper walked up to the stage. He got out a large piece of paper with a big drawing of a chicken shed on it and then started telling the parish council he would make sure the chicken cages were more comfortable than a luxury hotel room. A few people laughed when he said this but Sophie Pearce shot out of her chair and said 'LIAR!' and started telling everyone the true facts about battery chickens.

Eventually Anthea interrupted and said, 'I think that's enough, Sophie, some people have only just eaten.'

And Louise Fletton had to rush to the toilet to be sick.

Mr Draper snorted with laughter.

'The people of this parish may ALSO be interested to know,' he said, smirking at Sophie Pearce, 'that *if* I'm allowed to go ahead with the chicken farm, I will be giving away half a dozen eggs a week to every family in the parish – that's Muddlemoor AND Cudlington,' he added, winking at the members of the parish council who lived in Cudlington.

A few people started cheering and Mr Draper grinned.

'And,' he continued, 'I will sell my eggs to Mrs Rooney of Muddlemoor Stores at cost price – so she'll make money from the farm too. Everyone's a winner in Muddlemoor when it comes to my chickens.'

Mrs Rooney sat up and nodded at Mr Draper.

After that there were lots of long questions and there were even longer answers and I started getting a bit fidgety because sitting still in a meeting is not a Number One skill of mine. I felt in my jeans pocket to see if I had something to fiddle with, like for instance, the fidget spinner that the Bennett twins gave me for

Christmas, but, instead of the fidget spinner, I pulled out the coins that I had found in Mr Draper's field on Saturday. With the worry about Puff and then the excitement of the puppies, I had forgotten all about them. The six coins had been through the wash with my jeans and even though they were still a bit battered from being stuck in the mud, they gleamed in my hand.

I nudged Tom and Pip to let them know we'd be able to buy sweets later but Anthea looked at me and said, '*Shhhhh*,' so I held the coins tightly in my hand and pretended to listen.

'Can those members of the parish council AGAINST the chicken farm please raise their hands?' said Anthea.

Granny and Anthea's hands shot up and so did Mr Hodge's and Louise Fletton's.

'Four votes,' said Anthea, making a note.

'And can all members of the parish council IN FAVOUR of the chicken farm raise their hands?'

The four people from Cudlington put up their hands and so did Mrs Rooney.

Everybody started talking at the same time.

'Order, please!' said Anthea.

She cleared her throat.

'Five votes in favour and four against,' she said. 'This means the chicken farm can go ahead with immediate effect.'

A loud sobbing sound came from along our row of seats and when I looked over, I noticed that Sophie Pearce's face was wet with tears and her mum and dad had their arms around her.

Mr Draper stood up.

'I'd like to start by thanking the kind and sensible people of the parish council,' he said, and when he smiled I spotted lots of fillings at the back of his mouth. 'As soon as this wonderful new venture is up and running, people will be able to collect their boxes of eggs straight from the farm every weekend. I think we can all agree that care begins in the community and no one cares more about our community than me and Mrs Draper.'

Mrs Draper patted him on the back and said, 'Does this mean we can get that time share in Malta now, Fergal?'

Mr Draper nodded and lowered his voice, 'Keep *shtum* about that, Penny,' he said. 'Right now it's all about free eggs.'

Mrs Draper nodded and smiled.

'It's a travesty,' said Tom crossly, and I nodded, even though I didn't know what 'travesty' meant.

Granny and Mr Hodge stepped off the stage and walked over to us.

'Time to go home, you lot,' said Granny, swinging her handbag over her shoulder.

The handbag swung through the air and bumped into my arm, knocking the coins out of my hand.

'I'm so sorry, Joe,' said Granny as the coins clattered everywhere. 'I always forget what a brute this handbag is. What have you dropped?'

'Just a bit of money,' I said, bending down to pick it up. 'I found it the other day,' I explained to Tom and Pip.

One of the coins rolled along the floor towards Mr Hodge. When it reached his tatty old shoe, it fell over and stopped.

'What's this, Joseph?' said Mr Hodge.

'Joe,' I said. 'Not Joseph.'

But Mr Hodge didn't hear me. He bent down and picked up my coin. Instead of handing it to me, he stared at it and then he pulled his glasses out of his pocket.

'Erm, could I have my money back, please?' I said, because I was quite keen on getting to the shop to buy sweets as soon as possible.

'I don't believe it!' said Mr Hodge in a strange husky voice and then he started to laugh.

People who were starting to leave the village hall came back to find out what was happening.

'Anthony?' said Granny. 'Are you all right?'

Mr Hodge turned to Granny.

'I'm not sure,' he whispered. 'I feel rather faint.' He leaned on a chair. 'Can somebody get me a glass of water, please?'

Granny grabbed a jug of water from the table on the stage, poured some into a glass and brought it over to Mr Hodge. He drank the whole glass in one gulp.

'Joseph,' he said, all whispery, 'where did you find this, this . . . this fantastic artefact?'

'Joe!' I said, crossly. 'Not Joseph.' But Mr Hodge looked a bit strange, so I said, 'In Jeffrey's Meadow.' And then I gave him the other five coins.

A strange puffing sound started to echo around the village hall. At first I thought it was a gust of wind coming through one of the open windows and I even wondered if there was maybe a ghost who lived in the village hall but eventually I realised that it was just Mr Hodge hyperventilating. He clutched his chest, and Pip, who was filming everything, whispered that he might be having a heart attack because she'd seen one once on a TV programme called *Emergency Room*.

Anthea strode over with her clipboard. 'What on earth is the matter, Anthony?'

Mr Hodge held up my coins and swallowed. 'These,' he said, all breathless, '*these* are what's the matter.'

Anthea squinted.

'Little Joey found them in Jeffrey's Meadow.'

'*Joe*,' I muttered under my breath.

By now everybody had gathered round us to find

out what was going on.

Granny peered at the coins. 'But what ARE they, Anthony?'

Mr Hodge paused.

'If I'm not mistaken, these are solid gold sestertii from Hadrian's reign. They look to me like they may have been made by Antoninianos of Aphrodisius. Which would make them . . .' He swallowed. '. . . some of *the rarest and most unusual* Roman coins ever discovered.'

There was a long silence.

'Jeffrey's Meadow needs to be declared a site of national archaeological importance,' croaked Mr Hodge. 'Immediately.'

Sophie Pearce stopped sobbing and let out a long whistle. She walked over to us.

'Mr Hodge,' she said, staring at Mr Draper. 'Would you say that a site of national archaeological importance is a good place to build a battery chicken farm?'

'Good Lord, no!' said Mr Hodge, chuckling. 'No, no,

no. Chicken farms and archaeological digs are not a good mix. Not at all.'

Suddenly, a lot seemed to happen.

Mr Draper's face turned purple, Sophie Pearce fist-pumped the air and Mr Hodge had to lie down on the floor with his legs in the air.

Everybody came over to look at the coins, except Anthea who asked Sophie if she could borrow her phone.

Everything was starting to get quite noisy and out of hand, when the door of the village hall opened.

'Hi, there,' said a woman holding a camera. 'I'm Lisa Josephine from *Stonely News*. I've come to film a protest about a chicken farm. Have I got the wrong address?'

A man and another woman followed her into the hall. They were carrying bags and microphones.

Sophie leaped up.

'No!' she said. 'I'm Sophie Pearce, the person who sent you the videos. That's the man who wants to build the battery farm.' Sophie pointed to Mr Draper. 'The bad news is that he's just won the vote to build his chicken farm, but the good news is, this boy . . .' She pointed to me.

'Joe Robinson,' I said. 'J.O.E. Not Joseph, or Joey, just J—'

Sophie interrupted: '. . . has discovered rare and valuable Roman treasure on Jeffrey's Meadow. Which as you can imagine has put everything a bit up in the air!'

The woman with the camera grinned.

'Looks like we've got our story,' she said to a tall man carrying a camera bag, and then she started moving chairs and giving out orders.

Soon Lisa Josephine was interviewing Mr Hodge and Mr Draper and Sophie Pearce. She took some close-up footage of the six Roman coins and, finally, she interviewed me, Tom and Pip.

I told her the WHOLE story (although I didn't mention stealing the poison because Mr Draper was standing next to us and listening to every word).

'Puppies, too!' said Lisa Josephine. 'Excellent. Our viewers love a happy ending,' and then she got on the phone to her editor to ask if she could turn the news story into an hour-long feature.

At one point she asked if she could have a

look at some of the footage Pip had filmed on her video camera 'for authenticity'.

Pip said, 'Sure,' in a really calm voice but I could tell she was pleased because the tops of her cheeks turned pink.

The village hall was so noisy that nobody noticed a woman with long brown hair and dangly earrings arrive. Well, nobody except Anthea.

'Ah, Rachel!' said Anthea, striding over to the door. 'I was beginning to give up on you. Thanks for coming. The coins are over here.'

The woman called Rachel stepped carefully through the village hall. She wasn't very tall and she didn't look particularly interesting but at the same time everybody in the village hall stopped to look at her.

'What's the hold-up?' asked Lisa Josephine.

Anthea paused.

'This is my friend, Rachel Siddaway,' she announced. 'She is a professor of archaeology. I thought we could do with an expert round here. Just to ensure no monkey business takes place and everything is ticketyboo.'

Anthea glanced at Mr Draper and gave him the tiniest of smiles. Mr Draper scowled and walked over to Rachel Siddaway.

'I'm the owner of the field where the coins were found,' he said importantly. 'So that means they're my property, doesn't it?' Mr Draper lowered his voice and said, 'How much do you estimate a Roman haul like this fetches on the open market?'

Rachel Siddaway ignored Mr Draper and inspected the coins with a magnifying glass. After a few minutes, she cleared her throat and started to speak. 'These coins need to be placed in a museum for safekeeping,' she said. 'Without delay.' And even though her voice was quiet, EVERYBODY listened.

'Are they the real deal, then?' asked Lisa Josephine. 'Are they priceless Roman treasure?'

Rachel smiled.

'Yes,' she said, 'I believe they are significant.'

Immediately the cameras started whirring.

Anthony Hodge raced over to Rachel Siddaway and shook her hand.

'Fascinating to meet a fellow expert,' he said, and started telling her all about his own collection.

Mr Draper interrupted him.

'Those coins were found on my land,' he said. 'Which means they're MY property. What if I don't *want* you to take them away?'

Rachel Siddaway gave Mr Draper a serious look.

'I'm afraid it isn't up to you,' she said quietly. 'Until this case has been fully investigated, these coins are government property. And you're not allowed to build anything on that field until it has been thoroughly excavated.'

'But what about the time share in Malta?' wailed Mrs Draper. 'That's the only reason we wanted a chicken farm in the first place!'

'Shut up,' hissed Mr Draper.

Rachel smiled at them both.

'I appreciate that it must be tremendously exciting to

discover a treasure trove on your own land,' she said, 'but I'm afraid when it comes to an important find like this one, you're just going to have to be patient.'

'But I'm going to be rich, aren't I?' spluttered Mr Draper.

'Any payouts will need to wait until a proper investigation has been carried out,' said Rachel. 'My job now is to take these coins to a museum for safekeeping.'

As Rachel packed up the coins, the filming came to an end and people began to drift home. Eventually it was just us and Granny and Anthea and a lot of empty chairs.

Granny smiled. 'Are the heroes of the hour hungry?' she asked, and when we nodded she took us to Mrs Rooney's shop and let us choose a massive chocolate Easter egg each as a reward for stopping the battery chicken farm. I chose one with Maltesers inside but I remembered to check the best-before date on the packaging, because in Mrs Rooney's shop, you can't be too careful – especially when it comes to chocolate.

After that we went back to Granny's and ate so much chocolate, we didn't feel like eating lunch. But Granny said it didn't matter because she had forgotten to go to Sainsbury's.

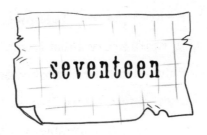

seventeen

S o that is pretty much the end of what happened at Granny's during the Easter holidays.

Things calmed down after the parish council meeting. For the next few days we spent a lot of time in the magnolia tree at the end of Granny's garden, watching the team of archaeologists excavate Jeffrey's Meadow.

Mr Draper came down to the site every day and spent ages quizzing the archaeologists about how much money they thought the treasure might be worth. He kept reminding them that he was the owner of the field. And the weird thing was, he seemed much less grumpy than before.

When we tried to return the bottles of Graingalore

to him (and admitted that we had stolen them), he barely heard us. 'Don't worry about it, kiddos,' he said cheerfully. 'I don't need to grow corn any more. Not now I won't have to feed any chickens. Give the fertiliser to your grandmother for her vegetable patch.' Then he leaned close and told us that an expert from the British Museum was arriving any day to value the treasure.

'They say it might be the find of the century,' he said, rubbing his hands together. 'Much more lucrative than battery farming. The wife and I might be able to *retire* to Malta, never mind a time share.'

'Good heavens,' said Granny when we handed over the Graingalore. 'I've never known Fergal Draper give anything away without wanting something in return. He must be expecting a VERY hefty payout for his Roman treasure. But tempting as it is, I can't possibly use Graingalore on my veg. Anthea would never forgive me.' And she put the black plastic bottles on a high shelf in the shed.

But later on that day, when Granny was drinking

tea and watching *Cul-de-Sac*, Pip climbed up to get one of the bottles. She poured a capful of Graingalore all over Granny's vegetable patch and winked at me and Tom. And we winked back, because keeping secrets from Anthea is fine with us, especially if it helps Granny win a prize for her vegetables.

The rest of the week flew by and it was nice not having to worry about chicken farms and people being poisoned. We kept an eye on the archaeologists and played the Boredom Cup and kicked a football – and we couldn't help noticing that Granny's broad beans were growing A LOT faster than usual.

On Thursday morning, Sophie Pearce called round to tell us that there was going to be a special report about Jeffery's Meadow after the Six O'Clock news.

That evening, Sophie, Anthea and Mr Hodge came round to watch it with us in Granny's sitting room. The special report was called *The Children Who Saved the Meadow* and it was all about us! It even included the videos of Sophie that Pip had filmed on her old camera and in the credits at the end it said: *Additional photography: Pip Berryman.*

I could tell that Pip was really pleased about this because she sat still for the whole thing.

She didn't do one single cartwheel or backflip. She didn't even do the splits.

When the film had finished, Sophie Pearce announced that she was taking things to the next level. 'This is just the beginning,' she said. 'My mission now is to persuade the government to ban ALL battery farms. I'm going to start up a massive petition and then I'm going to march to Ten Downing Street to present it to the Prime Minister.'

'Excellent gumption, young lady,' said Anthea, slapping Sophie on the back. 'What's the plan?'

Sophie spent a long time explaining her plan and then she asked me, Tom and Pip if we wanted to be part of the campaign. I wasn't a hundred per cent sure about saying yes because I knew that walking to Ten Downing Street would take a very long time (and one thing I'm not keen on is long walks) but Tom and Pip said yes straight away so I ended up agreeing with them.

On Friday morning, we went over to Sophie's

house to work on the new campaign. And although it wasn't *quite* as good as playing the Boredom Cup in the magnolia tree, it was actually OK, mainly because Sophie's parents are quite keen on giving away Bourbon biscuits – even when it's nearly lunchtime.

We were eating Bourbons and making *Chicken SOS* badges at Sophie's kitchen table, when the phone rang. Sophie's dad answered it and we couldn't help listening because a) we were right next to him and b) he kept talking about Jeffrey's Meadow.

When he got off the phone, he said, 'Blimey, THAT's a turn up for the books!' and then he explained that the person on the phone was a lawyer friend who had been looking into the Jeffrey's Meadow ownership documents.

'It turns out,' said Mr Pearce, 'that Mr Draper doesn't actually *own* Jeffrey's Meadow after all. That particular field happens to be common land.'

'What does that mean?' asked Sophie, making notes on her phone.

Mr Pearce took off his glasses and rubbed his eyes.

'It means,' he said slowly, 'that the field where Joe found the Roman treasure belongs to the whole village.'

We gasped and Sophie's dad laughed.

'The parish council created the documents years ago, way before Mr Draper bought Stream Farm. They were designed to prevent future farmers from selling Jeffrey's Meadow to building developers. But in this case, of course, it means that . . .' He looked at us and winked. '. . . Fergal Draper has to split any profits that come from the sale of the Roman treasure with every household in Muddlemoor!'

'NO WAY!' said Sophie, and straight away she started texting people.

'Not only that,' said Mr Pearce, smiling at me, 'but you, Joe, as the finder of the treasure will also get a share of the profits. I don't know how much exactly, but it could be as much as four figures.'

My heart started to bubble like crazy. I may not be a

genius at maths but even I knew that four figures was a fortune. For a while I couldn't speak. Instead, I started thinking of all the things I could spend the money on, starting with a zoo of my own. I couldn't wait to tell Mum and Bella. But first I needed to check something. I cleared my throat.

'Mr Pearce,' I said. 'Does this also mean that the owners of the field, i.e. all the people who live in Muddlemoor, can stop Mr Draper from building a chicken farm on Jeffrey's Meadow, even when the archaeologists have finished digging?'

Mr Pearce smiled at me.

'Well, Joe,' he said, 'it certainly looks that way.'

I started to cheer and the others joined in and eventually we found that we couldn't stop.

Soon, everybody in Muddlemoor was talking about Mr Pearce's lawyer friend's news and on Saturday practically the whole village met in The Old Boot to celebrate.

The only person NOT happy was Mr Draper.

According to Sophie Pearce, he spent the whole evening swearing and he drank so much beer, he passed out at his table. But nobody felt sorry for him because when he woke up he refused to pay for his drinks.

Then, on Easter Sunday, something EVEN MORE amazing happened. It was so exciting, it made us forget about chicken farms and Roman treasure and award-winning vegetables. It even made Tom forget about Sophie Pearce's anti-chicken battery farm campaign.

We were eating chocolate in Granny's garden when Bob and Sally Merry leaned over the hedge and asked if we wanted to come and see Puff's puppies. And we said yes like a shot because we had been waiting for them to ask for nearly a week.

Puff and her puppies were in a big cardboard box in the Merrys' kitchen. They looked like guinea pigs and they smelled of biscuits. They were INCREDIBLE.

Puff blinked at us and wagged her tail and I blinked back.

Four of the puppies were pure brown but one was

white with brown spots on its back. It was the only one with its eyes open and it looked right at me.

I asked Sally what they were going to do with the puppies and she said they were going to keep one for themselves and find wonderful for ever homes for the other four.

At that point I couldn't help remembering that even though our flat in London is quite small, there is DEFINITELY enough room in the kitchen for a

puppy. And I also couldn't help remembering about my treasure-finding money; suddenly I knew exactly what I was going to spend it on.

Later on, Tom and Pip agreed with me that there was enough room in our flat for a tiny puppy. They also agreed that it was a shame I didn't have one single true-life pet in my life. But then Tom pointed out that when it comes to puppies, parents can be a bit tricky.

'This kind of thing,' he said, 'requires proper planning.'

Tom turned to a brand-new page of his notebook.

First of all he wrote:

OPERATION PUPPY

And then he wrote:

How to smuggle a puppy to London

And after that we headed over to the weeping willow tree because we couldn't risk Granny or Anthea or the Merrys (or anybody else in Muddlemoor) finding out about our latest plan.

At least not until we had worked out
every
tiny
detail.

THE MUDDLEMOOR MYSTERIES

Granny's village is a hotspot for crime. Joe and his cousins have to concentrate even when they're watching telly. And the weird thing is, Granny never seems to notice.

Peril at the Bake Off --->

When Granny's precious cake recipe goes missing days before the Great Village Bake Off, Joe, Tom and Pip are FLABBERGASTED. They KNOW that one of the neighbours has stolen it but the question is, WHO?

<---- The Book Club Bank Heist

Granny's Book Group seems to be acting RATHER suspiciously. For one thing they NEVER talk about books and for another thing they keep going on about a local bank. Oh no! What if Granny's Book Group are true-life bank robbers?

The Chicken Farm Fiasco

The cousins join a protest group to try to stop Mr Draper's horrible battery chicken farm. But they soon notice that Mr Draper's enemies keep getting sick. Oh no! Is Mr Draper poisoning them? And, if so, is Granny in DANGER?